THE HEARTBREAKER

Recent Titles by Elisabeth McNeill from Severn House

THE SCOTTISH HISTORICAL SERIES

FLODDEN FIELD
BLOOD ROYAL
THE HEARTBREAKER

THE EYEMOUTH DISASTER STORIES

THE STORM
TURN OF THE TIDE

THE EDINBURGH MYSTERIES

HOT NEWS
PRESS RELATIONS

A BOMBAY AFFAIR
THE SEND-OFF
THE GOLDEN DAYS
UNFORGETTABLE
THE LAST COCKTAIL PARTY

DUSTY LETTERS
MONEY TROUBLES
TURN BACK TIME

THE
HEARTBREAKER

Prince Charles Edward Stewart

Elisabeth McNeill

This first world edition published 2009
in Great Britain and 2010 in the USA by
SEVERN HOUSE PUBLISHERS LTD of
9–15 High Street, Sutton, Surrey, England, SM1 1DF.

British Library Cataloguing in Publication Data

McNeill, Elisabeth.
  The Heartbreaker.
  1. Charles Edward, Prince, grandson of James II, King of
  England, 1720–1788 – Fiction. 2. MacDonald, Flora,
  1722–1790 – Fiction. 3. London (England) – History – 18th
  century – Fiction. 4. Biographical fiction.
  I. Title
  823.9'14–dc22

ISBN-13: 978-0-7278-6837-4   (cased)

All Severn House titles are printed on acid-free paper.

Severn House Publishers support The Forest Stewardship Council [FSC],
the leading international forest certification organisation. All our titles that
are printed on Greenpeace-approved FSC-certified paper carry the FSC logo.

Mixed Sources
Product group from well-managed
forests and other controlled sources
www.fsc.org Cert no. SA-COC-1565
© 1996 Forest Stewardship Council
FSC

Typeset by Palimpsest Book Prod
Grangemouth, Stirlingshire, Scotla
Printed and bound in Great Brita
MPG Books Ltd., Bodmin, Corn

Once again, I want to thank my wonderful researcher Alex Merry whose enthusiasm has kept me going throughout the writing of the book.

Prologue

On July 23rd 1745, Charles Edward Louis John Casimir Silvester Severino Maria Stewart jumped out of a small boat and waded up the beach at Eriskay, a tiny island off the coast of Barra in the Western Highlands of Scotland. When he reached dry land he threw his arms up in the air and gave a wild whoop of joy. 'I've come to claim my birthright!' he cried to the skies.

The seven men who accompanied him also yelled in support while, with a grandiose gesture, he reached into the pocket of his embroidered waistcoat and threw a scatter of tiny black seeds into the air. 'These will grow here to keep my memory alive forever,' he said.

Though he was to make many other unfulfilled predictions, this one came true. To this day a tiny wild type of periwinkle called the Prince's Flower grows on the Eriskay foreshore and nowhere else in Scotland.

The imposingly named young man, known to his supporters at the Young Chevalier and to his enemies as the Young Pretender, was of middle height, fair-haired and handsome with an attractive face and an athletic body. He was the twenty-five-year-old eldest son of the Jacobite Old Pretender, who claimed to be James III of England, Scotland, Ireland and Wales. His son landed in Eriskay to launch a rebellion on behalf of his father.

The trouble was that James did not want to be reinstalled on the throne of his ancestors. In 1715 he had made an abortive attempt to return to Scotland himself but retreated back to Rome after only two months. He was very much against his son's efforts to reignite his Jacobite claims.

Charles, however, was more quixotic and ignored his father's disapproval, setting off from France with a considerable fleet and soldiers supplied by Louis XV of France who was always eager to support any diversionary trouble on the English border. Unfortunately the fleet ran into storms and most of the ships were either wrecked or returned to France. Only two, the *Elisabeth* and the *Doutelle*, made it to Scotland. The Young Chevalier was on board the *Doutelle*.

When he walked ashore at Eriskay there were seven loyal Jacobites, mostly Irishmen, with him and only a few supporters waiting to welcome him ashore. The clan chiefs and Highland magnates were holding back, reluctant to pledge support till they found out whether he was likely to have any success, or copy his father and hightail it back to France after the first setback.

He met with a better response when he managed to sail across to Moidart, just north of the Sound of Mull. There, on August 19th, he and his seven supporters, known thereafter as the Seven Men of Moidart, raised the Jacobite standard on a point of land sticking out into the sea at Glenfinnan.

Supporters gradually arrived from the Highlands and Islands to join him. He had immense charm when he chose to turn it on and was particularly popular with women, though it is likely that when he landed in Scotland he was still a virgin, an unusual state for a royal prince, even a pretender, by the age of twenty-five.

In spite of his handsomeness and charm there was a dark side to Charles Edward, for he was pathologically selfish, extremely arrogant and careless about other people's feelings. At the age of five he refused to bow to the Pope because, as he explained, Popes were only elected while *he* was born a prince.

Though musical, and fluent in four languages, he was not a good scholar and had little interest in learning. Any letters he wrote in English were almost illiterate. In fact, when he was growing up, gossip reached the Hanoverian court that he was an imbecile and his father always bemoaned his lack of learning. Also, and most tellingly, by the time he landed in Scotland he was already drinking heavily, with a marked partiality for brandy.

In 1745 however, his romantic charm prevailed among many pro-Jacobites in the Highlands and excitement and enthusiasm for his cause increased. His followers grew in number till he was heading a small army by early September when they reached Perth before marching into a stunned Edinburgh on the 17th of the month.

When he held court in Holyrood Palace, more men, mostly Highlanders, flocked to join him and on the 21st of the month

– after a fifteen-minute battle at Prestonpans a few miles south of Edinburgh – an English army under Sir John Cope was roundly defeated by his forces. The delighted Jacobites celebrated this victory by singing a derisory song, 'Hey Johnnie Cope are ye sleepin' yet?'

For five more weeks, Bonnie Prince Charlie, as he was by then popularly called, stayed on in Edinburgh dispensing charm and gathering a bigger army, still mainly made up of Highlanders for there was only half-hearted support for him from Edinburgh and the east coast of Scotland or the Lothians.

In spite of that, he managed to gather an army of 5,500 men before marching into England, going first to Carlisle and then Manchester. Both cities fell with little opposition, thanks to the brilliant general Lord George Murray who, after some hesitation, had declared himself on Charles Edward's side. Unfortunately he and Charles were on bad terms from the beginning because Murray mistrusted the younger man's judgement and Charles was suspicious of him, fearing that he might be a traitor.

By the first week of December they reached the outskirts of Derby, only 120 miles from London. There they unexpectedly halted and, to general Jacobite dismay, retreated in disarray. For the rest of his life the Young Chevalier blamed Murray for turning back and always said that he himself wanted to press on but was overruled by Murray who insisted on retreating because their lines of communication were stretched too far and he felt they could easily be cut off.

Charles, and many other people, believed that if the Jacobite army had pressed on, he could have taken London. Spies told him that the Hanoverian King George II had actually made plans to load his personal treasures into a boat and flee down the Thames and back to Hanover as soon as the Jacobite army reached London.

Sadly the retreat from Derby was a total debacle during which many of Charles' army were slaughtered or made prisoners. By Christmas Day, the remnants were in Glasgow, where the prince met a merchant's daughter called Clementine Walkinshaw who nursed him when he fell ill at Bannockburn and later became his mistress. She was to bear his daughter Charlotte.

On January 17th Murray won a skirmish against the Hanoverian army at Falkirk but the tide had turned too decisively. The only thing to do was retreat northwards pursued by the English Red-coat army under the King's son, the Duke of Cumberland. By early spring the remnants of the Jacobite army were in Inverness, weary, underfed and over tired.

On April 17th, they were overwhelmed on Culloden Moor with the loss of 2000 men. Charles and a few supporters fled the field early and left his supporters to their cruel fate. Many were slaughtered while they slept from exhaustion and hunger. The few who were not killed were either cruelly executed later, or sent to prison ships in the Thames and ended up as slaves in the American colonies. The Duke of Cumberland has gone down in history with the nickname of The Butcher because of the terrible cruelties he inflicted on Charles' supporters and their families after Culloden.

Murray escaped to the Continent and was received at the court of Charles' father James in Rome. He and Charles never met again and Murray died in Holland in 1760 at the age of sixty-six.

Charles, hoping to be rescued by a French ship, went on the run in the Western Isles with a handful of his original supporters. A £30,000 reward was offered for his capture. In an exhausted and tattered condition, he ended up on the island of Raasay where, on July 1st, he was passed into the care of a young woman called Flora Macdonald who was sleeping in a bothy while looking after a flock of sheep for her brother.

The Macdonalds were ostensibly on the government side but, like many Highland families, secretly sympathetic to the Jacobite cause and Flora's stepfather sent her a letter ordering her to smuggle the Young Chevalier across to Skye so that he could pick up the French ship that was waiting for him off the mainland coast.

At first Flora refused to take on such a responsibility, but when she actually saw the young prince, who was ragged, filthy and exhausted, she felt she had to help him, as she herself later said she would have helped anyone in such a parlous situation.

It took her twelve days to get him safely off Skye, and for part of the time he was unconvincingly disguised as her Irish maid-servant Betty Burke. On September 20th he sailed away from

Arisaig on a French ship called *L'Esperance*. He never came back to Scotland though he talked about returning many times and regarded his trek across Skye as the most exciting episode of his life . . .

One

1750

When Flora saw him in the Strand, she gasped and staggered a little so that her companion Lady Primrose took hold of her arm and whispered, 'Yes, it's our Prince. Don't stare. Don't attract attention to him.'

An unbidden thought came into her head. *But he wants attention. He always wants to be noticed and admired.* As she stared across the highway at him she was suddenly filled with the feeling of having all her illusions wrenched away from her. It was as if she was able truly to judge him for the first time.

In her heart of hearts, however, she knew that she had been critical of him from the beginning but had not allowed herself to acknowledge her doubts.

'What is he doing here?' she whispered back to Lady Primrose who was still holding tightly on to her.

'Meeting his followers. They call themselves the Royal Oak Society and they meet at the Crown and Anchor Inn just over there.' When Lady Primrose nodded her head towards the other side of the Strand, her eyes were aglow with adoration.

'But the authorities . . . What would they do if they knew he was here?'

'They know. Of course they know. They're afraid to challenge him because he's too popular. Half of London would rise up on his behalf if he gave the signal.'

Flora stared into her companion's face and saw that her ladyship really believed what she was saying. For herself, she suspected that the authorities were well aware Prince Charles Edward Stewart was in London but would do nothing because he was no longer significant. They could afford to treat him with scorn because he was no danger to them any more. Tears sprang into her eyes when she remembered all the gallant, true men who'd died or were driven from their homes for his cause.

She stared across the roadway at him again and thought angrily, 'You left devastation behind you in the Highlands. Men were slaughtered or tortured, women raped, and houses burned down. And yet here you are, posturing like a dandy.'

She herself had been captured, thrown into a prison ship, then shut up in the Tower of London and threatened with execution or enslavement on his behalf. She only escaped by the skin of her teeth. Yet he was on the other side of the Strand, decked out in brocade and lace with a powdered wig and buckled shoes with high red heels, throwing his hands about and making a lot of noise. *Drunk again probably*, she thought with a surge of scorn and dislike that rose in her throat like acid.

The anger that filled her had to be hidden, however, because she had no wish to upset kind Lady Primrose who worshipped the Prince. She had been immensely good to Flora and from the beginning had lobbied on her behalf, saving her life and transforming her fortunes. It was Lady Primrose who made her famous as the Prince's saviour though she had not sought or rejoiced in that fame. Obscurity suited her better. It was a lot less hazardous.

'You must be worried for his safety now he's in London,' she said to her kind companion whose pretty face was still shining with delight.

'I'm in heaven whenever I see him. He's staying in my house with his friend Captain Brett, and people are coming from near and far to kneel before him. This morning the house was full because he's been touching poor souls for the King's Evil too. God grant that the poor sick people get a cure,' she said.

Flora could imagine the scene with Charles basking in the regard of his admirers while credulous ladies in fine silk dresses with Jacobite white roses in their hair ushered in sick people with horrible scrofula marks on their necks and faces. She doubted very much if there would be many cures, however.

'What about Culloden?' That was what she would want to ask him if they met again. 'What about the clansmen who dropped to their knees for want of food and were slaughtered where they lay? What about the starving families of men sold into slavery? What about the unrewarded boatmen who rowed you to safety and were tortured and killed by the English because of their loyalty to you? What about me?'

Fortunately Lady Primrose knew nothing of those angry thoughts but she was concerned because Flora was showing obvious signs of emotion.

Of course, the poor girl's upset. She must have fallen deeply in love with the Prince while they were on the run in Skye. She probably still adores him. After all, who isn't in love with the Young Chevalier? These were the thoughts of Lady Primrose, who could not imagine anyone failing to adore her Prince.

She wished she could tell Flora to forget him because her love was doomed to disappointment. When he married it would have to be to a woman of noble birth, a princess at the very least. She resolved to put her mind to finding Flora a suitable husband. The girl was twenty-eight, after all, and although unfortunately quite plain, she was well bred by Highland standards for her father had been a landowner. But she was certainly not well enough bred to aspire to be the wife of Prince Charles Edward Stewart.

But she had been very brave, and certainly saved his life. Lady Primrose deliberately quelled any disappointment that she felt because after the Prince left Skye and was safe in France, he made no effort to reward Flora or anyone else who helped him. When they parted all he gave her was a handful of small coins because at one stage in their journey she'd lent him a florin.

When she heard that, Lady Primrose had been energized into rectifying the oversight on his part and collected money from her Jacobite friends to reward the girl who had saved the life of their Prince. They were thrilled by the thought that she'd dressed him up as her maidservant Betty Burke and bravely took him across Skye under the noses of the redcoats. It was a brave thing to do because she'd certainly have been killed if the English found them.

Lady Primrose's fund-raising had provided Flora with the considerable sum of fifteen hundred pounds, a fortune by Raasay standards. When it was given to her, Flora's face went white and then red. 'But I didn't do it for money!' she exclaimed.

'My dear, you well deserve the money,' said Lady Primrose who knew that with such a large sum at her disposal, Flora had the chance of making a decent marriage. Gossip had it that her villainous stepfather, One-Eyed Hugh Macdonald, certainly would not pay to marry her off and she had nothing of her own. Her father died too young to make proper provision for his daughter.

Seeing that Flora was still staring across the Strand at the Prince, her ladyship took a firmer hold of the girl's elbow and hustled her along to stop her attracting bypassers' attention to him. In spite of what she said about the authorities being scared to challenge him, she did not fully believe it. It was common knowledge that a network of spies followed him everywhere he went and reported back both to the Hanoverian authorities and to his disapproving father in Rome. The spies had even infiltrated her own household but she could do nothing about it. There was no point.

'Come along now, Flora. You'll see him face to face again tomorrow,' she said firmly.

Flora turned her head and asked in wide-eyed surprise, 'Me? See him tomorrow? How? Where?'

'At my house in Essex Street. I'm holding a reception for him and he's *longing* to see you.'

This last part was a lie but only a little one. In fact he hadn't mentioned Flora's name since he arrived three days ago but she was sure that if he heard she was coming to the reception, he would be pleased to see her again and thank her for her efforts on his behalf.

Flora shook her head when she heard this and said, 'That's a pity because I can't come to Essex Street tomorrow, Your Ladyship. I'm going back to Scotland in the morning.'

'So soon? But you only arrived in London three days ago. Are your rooms at the inn uncomfortable? I'm sorry I couldn't put you up in my house but I knew the Prince was coming with all his people and there wasn't enough room . . .'

'Oh no; I'm very happy with my accommodation but I have to go back now because . . . because I had a letter from my mother this morning to tell me I've had an offer.'

'What sort of an offer?'

'An offer of marriage.'

Lady Primrose clasped her hands in delight when she heard this and cried out, 'Oh my dear, that is what I most wanted for you. How exciting! Who is it from?'

'Allan Macdonald.'

Even though her ladyship had strong Scottish connections, for her late husband was a member of one of the most powerful families, she preferred to stay in London, far away from her native country. As a result she always found it difficult to cope with the multitude of people who shared a surname but seemed to know exactly where they all fitted in to the intricate spiders' web network. There were hundreds of Macdonalds, for example – all so interconnected that it was impossible to tell who was important and who was not.

'At least you won't be changing your surname if you marry your suitor. You'll still be the famous Flora Macdonald!' she said, nodding enthusiastically, and adding, 'That's good!' as she waited to be told more.

'Allan's father is the factor for Macdonald of Sleat. He lives in a fine house called Kingsburgh on Skye,' Flora told her.

That was not a lot of help either but Lady Primrose obviously wanted more details, so Flora went on, 'He's about two years older than me and very handsome. I've seen him from a distance but never thought he'd look at me. My stepfather arranged it all and he thinks it's a good match.'

As she spoke they were both thinking about the incentive of her sizeable dowry but Lady Primrose was still delighted and cried, 'I can see you like the idea of marrying this Allan! Go north with my blessing, my dear. I'll tell the Prince your news and I'm sure he'll be happy for you, too.'

Arriving back at the White Hart Inn where she had rooms, Flora rushed in and told her maid Chrissie, 'Pack our traps, we're going home tomorrow.'

Usually nothing fazed Chrissie but this time she asked, 'Is it because of the letter that came from your mother this morning? You've only just got here. What's the hurry?'

'One reason is because Betty Burke's in town and I don't want to meet him again.'

'The Stewart Prince, you mean? He's in London?' Chrissie was astonished by this news.

'Yes. I saw him in the Strand half an hour ago.'

'Did he see you?'

'No.'

'That's a good thing. You don't want any more trouble by

involving yourself with him again. The last time you ended up
in prison and nearly lost your life. You mightn't get away with it
a second time. It's best to go back home and keep out of his
way. If they catch him they'll have his head off and you don't
want to be thrown back in the Tower, do you?' the maid said as
she hurriedly began folding up clothes.

'I agree. But I don't think the government really cares what
he does any more. It's only Lady Primrose and her friends who
are interested in him now and I don't want to join in while they
fawn over him. I know too much about him, you see.'

Chrissie scowled. Her husband had been one of the boatmen
who rowed the Prince away from Skye and he died of his ill
treatment by the English soldiers who captured him after Charles
escaped to France. Any Jacobite sympathies she'd once held were
long dead.

Flora went on, 'But there's another reason why I'm not going
to meet him tomorrow. You were right about my mother's letter.
She says that Allan Macdonald's made an offer for me and I've
decided to accept him.'

Chrissie stared intently into the other's face looking for signs
about how Flora felt about this offer. 'Allan? That's the black-
haired handsome fellow whose father's Kingsburgh's factor, isn't
it? He's a bonnie-looking man, right enough,' she said carefully,
all the time trying to recall what she knew of him.

He was handsome indeed, and popular with everybody because
of his open, friendly nature, but he was reputed to be lazy at
work and not very canny or calculating when it came to making
business decisions. Like his father, he hadn't openly declared
himself one way or another during the 1745 rising. In fact he'd
signed up on the English side and wore the red coat of
Cumberland's soldiers though he was never actually involved in
any fighting so nobody was too antagonized.

Chrissie loved Flora and she thought that Allan Macdonald
would be the one getting the best side of the bargain as the
sensible lassie would probably make a man of him. 'He's a bonnie-
looking man and he'll give you braw bairns,' she said cautiously.

Flora gave a little laugh. 'He's good breeding stock, you mean!'

'There's nothing wrong with that. We need good men to replace
the ones we've lost,' Chrissie told her seriously.

Two

When Lady Primrose brought up Flora's name that evening, Prince Charles Edward looked blank for a moment and she had to remind him of the girl who'd spent twelve days helping him to escape from Cumberland's men on Skye.

'Oh yes,' he said. 'There were so many Macdonalds. I remember that girl. She was always so stern. I don't think she liked me.'

Lady Primrose laughed her tinkling laugh and said, 'Like all of us, she was in love with you, Your Highness, and probably still is!'

He preened and laughed back and she wished she had the courage to ask him if it was true that he and Flora had shared a bed at one stage of their adventure but even she did not dare to take that liberty.

'How is she?' he asked.

'Very well now but she was in much trouble after you escaped. She was shipped down here as a prisoner and kept in the Tower for over a year. Cumberland wanted her to be executed or transported as a slave but she's got a good head on her and she kept cool and made a very good impression on many influential people, especially on the Prince of Wales. He would not let his butcher brother take his vengeance out on her.'

Charles looked horrified at this, as if he was hearing about the atrocities heaped on his supporters for the first time. 'She didn't suffer too much I hope,' he said.

Lady Primrose hastened to reassure him. 'No, sire. When she got out of the Tower, I brought her here to stay with me and she was officially pardoned in 1747. All your supporters made much of her. In fact she was the toast of the town, moving so much in high society that her manners and looks were much improved. She even had her portrait painted by Alan Ramsay and she went to learn writing in Edinburgh. She became a real lady.'

'That's good. She'd never have had those advantages if she'd stayed on Raasay,' he said coolly.

Lady Primrose seized the chance to remind him that he had not rewarded Flora for her help and said, 'Your supporters in London raised a fund for her – we got one thousand five hundred pounds.'

He was unabashed. 'That's a fair sum for a girl like her. She was sleeping in a sheep bothy when I first saw her.' He did not choose to remember that if Flora had betrayed him and told the English about his whereabouts, she could have earned herself the far larger reward of thirty thousand pounds that was offered to anyone who turned him in.

Lady Primrose nodded. 'At least she'll be able to find a good husband now. Her stepfather, One-Eyed Hugh Macdonald of Armadale, is a tight-fisted miser who won't give a farthing to marry her off but now she has a big enough dowry to make a decent marriage. In fact she told me yesterday that she's about to take a husband.'

'It sounds as if you like the girl,' said Charles.

'I do. She deserves credit for saving you, sire. If she hadn't done what she did Cumberland's men would have captured you.'

He waved an airy hand. 'Oh, I don't think so. The French would have got me out eventually. I was sure I'd get away, but she did help a little.'

Even the hero-worshipping Lady Primrose was shocked by this careless acceptance of what had been done for him – but she excused him because after all he was a Prince, born to be confident that nothing could ever threaten him.

Three

In her sister's rooms in St James' Palace, Clementine Walkinshaw clenched her hands tightly as she hissed, 'Are you absolutely sure he's in London?'

Her sister Catherine was taken aback by Clementine's intensity and said, 'Yes, I'm sure. It's common knowledge apparently. My lady the Princess and her friends were talking about him this morning. He goes openly to meet his friends at an ale house in the Strand and Lady Primrose is giving a reception for him tomorrow night. Even some of our court ladies are going. Everyone's mad with curiosity to see him.'

Clementine said urgently, 'I have to go too. I must! I must!'

Catherine put her hands on her younger sister's shaking shoulders and said, 'I don't think you should. You've made a mistake once; don't make another.'

'You don't understand. I'd die for him if he asked me to. You must get me into Lady Primrose's reception!'

'How can I do that?'

'You know everybody. Ask one of the Princess of Wales' friends to take me in her party. You know lots of people who keep a foot in both camps. Wales favours the Jacobite supporters because he hates his brother Cumberland so much and you're one of his wife's Ladies of the Bedchamber. If you can't get me into the Primrose house, no one can.'

'If I do, promise me you won't do anything stupid or make a scene. You must promise me that.'

'I promise. I only want to see him again, to kiss his hand and tell him that I still love him.'

Catherine sighed. Her youngest sister's devotion to Charles Edward Stewart perplexed her because, judging from everything she had heard in the Hanoverian court, he was a drunken fop and a failure, but to help Clementine she called in a few favours in the Court of St James and an invitation was issued for the Primrose reception.

On the next evening Clementine didn't look her thirty years after Catherine dressed her dark hair high and crowned it with a coronet of Jacobite green acorns that matched her silk gown. Her eyes sparkled with excitement when a hand mirror was held up before her and she twirled on her toes before she kissed her sister and said, 'Thank you, thank you, Catherine. You'll never know how much this means to me.'

Catherine was more circumspect. 'Hang on to your common sense, Clemmie. He's been very unlucky for you before. Don't let that happen again.'

'He couldn't come back for me after Culloden. It wasn't his fault. He doesn't know what happened. I wanted to tell him about the baby but it was impossible. He doesn't know about it. No one does except our family.'

'From what I hear he hasn't let memories of you hold him back from having affairs with other women. They say that in spite of his father's disapproval he's been living in Avignon with an opera singer from Paris for a long time and there are other women in his life too.'

Clementine was unperturbed. 'All women adore him. It's not his fault. They pursue him but it's me that he loves. I know it. I'm certain of it.'

Catherine pulled a disapproving face. 'Stop talking nonsense. If he loved you so much, he'd at least have sent you one message in four years, wouldn't he?'

But Clementine refused to let her sister take the thrill out of her excitement. She was going to see the man she adored. Who knew what would happen as a result of their meeting?

The huge reception room in Essex Street was packed full of people, men and women pressed up close together, the shorter ones craning their necks and standing on tiptoe to catch a glimpse of the Prince. The scent of heavy perfume mingled with the stronger smell of body sweat, proving that even the finest bred people in the land could smell as strong as goatherds in the steamy heat of a warm September evening.

Charles Edward Louis John Casimir Sylvester Severino Maria Stewart paraded among his people with a glass of brandy in his hand, sipping from it all the time and holding it out to be refilled every time it was half empty. He loved having been given so many fine names at his baptism and sometimes thought of himself as John or Casimir or Sylvester so that he could play the part of being someone else.

That night in Essex Street he felt there was not a man in the world more daring, more fortunate or more deserving of adoration than himself. Everybody loved him; they hung on each word he uttered as if it came from the mouth of a great philosopher and he preened himself when they called him the Young Chevalier.

As far as he was concerned, he had committed no errors, made no mistakes, let no one down. The mistake of turning back at Derby and then running away from Culloden was erased from his mind. Those decisions had not been his to make. They were the fault of other people, especially that dastard Murray. Let him take the blame.

When his querulous father, who had been against the '45 expedition from the beginning, wrote him letters of reproach, he never answered but threw them away with a curl of the lip. The old man was in no position to criticize anybody because his own attempt at leading a rising in Scotland in 1715 was a fiasco and never really got started.

At least he, the Young Chevalier, took his men to Derby in the heart of England, and if it had not been for bad advice, perhaps even treacherous advice, he could have prevailed and taken London.

It was bittersweet to be in London now, knowing that it could have been his. Yesterday he'd gone to visit the Tower of London, walked to and fro and remarked very loudly to one of the guards how easy it would be to blow up the gates. The man had looked hard at him and laughed as if he was a fool, not taking him seriously. If he'd known he was talking to the rightful King that would have stopped him laughing.

Since his escape from Scotland, Charles had chosen to stay away from his permanently critical father, who languished in Rome scrawling out angry, despairing letters bemoaning that his heir was prancing about, spending too much money, and was still unmarried at the age of thirty.

In spite of these entreaties, he refused to go to see the old man and would not grieve if they never met again because he did not care for criticism. What business was it of his father's if he spent money? There was plenty, wasn't there? They were rich though the old man always pleaded penury and lived like a miser though he owned much of the English Crown jewels that *his* father had spirited out of England, as well as the jewels and fortune of his wife, Princess Clementina Sobieski, daughter of the King of Poland, who'd given birth to Charles Edward.

What business was it of his father if the son drank a little too much now and again? A man had to relax and forget his worries, hadn't he? What business was it of his father if he took up with temperamental or low-class women? They amused him.

He did not want to get married and the possible brides suggested for him were all unappealing. It seemed that the parents of any high-born young and pretty princesses were none too keen to ally their daughters with a Stewart in exile. If the Czarina of Russia was prepared to accept him, he'd think about marrying *her*, but he was not prepared to demean himself with less important women like the lumpy daughters of German margraves who were suggested to him.

Anyway, thought Charles, his father should stop complaining and be relieved that at least one of his sons was a normal man who knew what to do with a woman. His other son, Henry Benedict – only two names were given to him when he was christened – preferred to be fawned over and bedded by handsome young men. He'd been made a cardinal because the church seemed the best place for him. Left to Henry, the royal Stewart line would die out pretty quickly.

These thoughts were running through the Prince's head as he paraded before the admiring throng in Essex Street, and he did not notice Clementine Walkinshaw when she stood shyly in the room entrance, staring about in search of familiar faces.

She knew several of the people clustered by the main door and held her head proudly high as she passed them though she saw several stare and whisper behind their hands at the sight of her.

I have every right to be here, she told herself. *After all, I come from a good Jacobite family. My uncle kept the Prince in his home before Culloden. My father supported the Prince's father in 1715; he fought at Sheriffmuir and was exiled for his trouble. That's why I'm called*

Clementine because I was named after the Old Pretender's wife Clementina who my father met and much admired.

A woman from Edinburgh, one of the Macleods, put a hand on her arm and said, 'You're the youngest Walkinshaw girl, aren't you? I hope you're not here spying on your sister's behalf, Miss Walkinshaw.'

Clementine spun round and said angrily, 'My sister has nothing to do with where I go or who I see.'

'But she's the Princess of Wales' Woman of the Bedchamber, isn't she?'

'That has nothing to do with me.'

'Then be careful who you talk to about this. We don't want our Prince ending up in the Tower, do we?' said the woman, turning pointedly away.

Angrily Clementine pushed on through the mob. Though she was small and slight she could be as forceful as a battering ram. Nothing was going to stop her reaching him. At last she caught a glimpse of a laughing crowd at the far end of the room and her heart gave a lurch in her chest when she spotted him, resplendent in his fine embroidered clothes and powdered wig. His patrician face still looked boyish, and was as handsome as she remembered. His imperious nose was high bridged, his eyes full and roguish, and there was a humourous curve to his lips that made him look as if he was always on the brink of bursting into happy laughter. Bonnie Prince Charlie, the Highlanders had called him, and they were right. He was the bonniest man she'd ever seen.

With the strength of pure determination, she pushed on towards him, treading on strangers' toes and pushing disapproving people aside as she went.

'My prince,' she said in a voice of rapture, sinking in a deep curtsey when she found herself in front of him at last.

For a moment he looked nonplussed, as if he did not know her, but when she lifted her head and stared into his eyes, recognition dawned and he said formally, 'Miss Walkinshaw. Don't you look fine. It's a pleasure to see you here.' She held out a hand which he grasped and gently pulled her to her feet. 'Clementina,' he said in a softer voice. It was his mother's name and he had a major mother fixation, for she had left his father's household when he was only five years old and for ever after he feared that she had abandoned him.

Clementine did not take her hand from his though he uncurled his fingers. 'I have news for you, Your Highness,' she whispered and looked over her shoulder to the curving stairway where she hoped it would be possible for them to sit and speak in private.

'News?' he asked.

'About your family,' she told him.

'Let us sit down then and I will hear your news,' he replied and walked away with her while the assembled worshippers stared after them before bursting into a gabble of gossip.

'That's the youngest Walkinshaw girl. There are ten of them!'

'Her father was a textile mill owner and he was out in 1715. He's dead now but left his girls good dowries. This one's never married, though they say she shared the Prince's bed at her uncle's house in Bannockburn when he stayed there after Derby. I wonder if it's true . . .'

Unabashed, the curious turned and stared after the couple as they climbed halfway up the stairs and sat down together. The Prince did not mind the scrutiny, for he was used to it, but Clementine was more self-conscious and held her cupped hand over her lips as she whispered to him, 'The baby died, sire.'

Obviously surprised, he stared at her. 'What baby?'

'Our baby. It was but two hours old.'

'Our baby! When?'

'The same week as Culloden. I went to the country to have it but it died.'

He leaned forward and whispered urgently, 'Was it a male child?'

She nodded and he leaned back as if in exaltation, saying, 'So I can breed sons if I want to! I'm not sterile like Henry. You're sure it was mine?'

She was too besotted to take offence at this question. 'The child was yours,' she assured him and he grasped her hand.

'Thank you for telling me.'

'I love you,' said she softly and he looked at her now as if he was seeing her for the first time. She was no dashing beauty but open-faced and honest-looking, very Scottish in features, the child of a manufacturer without a drop of aristocratic blood. But she had carried his son.

His brother Henry often hinted that neither of them would ever be able to produce a child because they were of the same persuasion, men who preferred making love to other men rather than to women and, in truth, the idea of sex with women was not a great driving force for Charles either. He liked having women around when he needed them but he preferred the company of men. But this plain-faced girl had shared his bed and conceived his son. If she had done it once she could do it again.

It was unfortunate that the child died but it would have been impossible to acknowledge it if it had lived. To have a son, however, would stop Henry's malicious tongue and delight his father, who was brooding in deep disapproval of his oldest son's unwilling-ness to start a family and produce an heir for the Stewart line.

'I love you,' Clementine said again in a voice full of utter conviction and intensity.

He did not say he loved her back. Instead he said, 'Why don't you meet me in France? We could set up together.'

Her face flushed scarlet. Her skin was very white and he saw the tide of red colour seep down her cheeks to her neck and into her cleavage. It was obvious she would do anything he wanted. She'd always been very obliging.

He remembered being sick with exhaustion and a fever after coming back from Derby and she'd nursed him with mustard poultices and hot drinks at her uncle Hugh Paterson's house at Bannockburn. When he began to feel better he'd coaxed her into bed beside him, not from any great desire but because he needed relief.

'I'll go anywhere with you,' she told him in an even fiercer voice.

He smiled. He found it difficult to be totally drawn to any woman and the idea of falling hopelessly in love or doting on a wife or mistress seemed stupid. The only woman who'd ever truly captured his heart had been his mother but she'd taken to reli-gion and turned away from him when he was small. She'd made him very angry by her desertion.

Perhaps it was of significance that his mother and this girl shared a name. Clementina Sobieski and Clementine Walkinshaw. She would suit him very well. There would be no tantrums with her like his opera singer, no jealous fits like his other occasional mistresses, no grim disapproval of his little failings that was shown by the Flora Macdonald woman who'd bullied him around Skye.

He stood up and smiled down at her before speaking in his characteristically stilted way as if he was translating from the many languages that seemed to jumble around in his head. 'I must go back to my people now but I'll send a messenger to you and he will arrange how it can be done. Trust me,' he said.

Then he stepped elegantly back down the stairs into the watching throng while she stared after him wondering if he meant it. Did he really want her to go away with him? Would they really be together? Did he love her? She accepted that it was impossible for him to love her as much as she loved him, but now it seemed possible that he wanted her enough to take her as his mistress even if not as his wife. She made up her mind to go with him, no matter which it was.

Still vivid in her memory was the night she shared his bed at Bannockburn. She'd never slept with anyone before and was very timid but he reassured her and the actual act had been swiftly accomplished. So swift that later she found it almost impossible to believe that he'd impregnated her that night – on the only occasion they slept together.

She carried the child to full term and her sisters managed to keep the birth a secret by hiding her away in their homes when she began to show unmistakeable signs of pregnancy and they arranged for her to be delivered in a house belonging to one of their friends in the Lake District.

Her labour was hard and the poor little thing was born blue, dying before it was able to breathe properly. Her sisters buried the little corpse in the garden. They were trying to protect her because if she was known to have borne a child it would prejudice her chance with any other suitor, but they did not realize that there was no one else in the world that she would ever love or want to be with except Bonnie Prince Charlie.

When Charles re-entered the reception room he was already drunk and his head was swimming but he took another sip of brandy and tried to remember that he'd have to do something about that girl who'd just told him she'd conceived his son. He'd asked her to join him in France, hadn't he? Tomorrow he must find someone to take care of that problem and arrange the details. If she produced another son for him, he might even marry her. That would surely satisfy his father, though he'd be horrified about the child having a mother of such low birth, but it might stop him being so critical and disapproving all the time. No wonder his mother had given herself up to religion.

There was something else he was determined to do before he left London – something that would horrify his father even more. He intended to renounce the Roman Catholic faith and join the Church of England. He'd already arranged to take the step tomorrow morning in the church of St Mary le Strand, though he was not entirely sure why.

Perhaps one reason was because he knew that news of his conversion might send his father into a seizure and horrify his brother Henry. Another was because of advice from his Jacobite supporters who backed up his plans to make another attempt at restoring the Stewart dynasty. They said English people would rally to him more eagerly if he adopted the Protestant faith. His father's staunch and rigorous Roman Catholicism frightened many of them off, for they did not want another Catholic on the English throne.

He took another swig of his brandy and enjoyed a vainglorious image of himself taking to the field again, this time at the head of a victorious army. After all he was the true heir. Those Germans from Hanover were only usurpers.

Smiling, he stepped into a throng of admiring people who opened up a way for him as if he was Moses cutting through the Red Sea. They loved and admired him and he lived for the moment, wallowing in their love.

Four

When Flora and Chrissie reached Edinburgh they slept a night in an inn at the bottom of the Cowgate before Flora went to meet her mother Marion at the townhouse of their clanswoman, Lady Macdonald of Borrodale.

Her ladyship was in the hall when Flora arrived at the house in the High Street and sneered when she saw the young woman. 'So you're back. They tell me you're marrying our factor's son. He's only taking you because of the money those silly women in London collected for you. You've done well out of the Stewart pretender but not everyone has been so lucky.'

Flora knew better than to answer that for she was well aware that Lady Macdonald hated her and called her 'that gypsy' because she blamed Flora for putting her family in danger by taking the Prince to her house on Skye. When they arrived she was prepared to help him, and although she did not want to receive him in the house, she supplied him with liberal amounts of brandy.

Her husband was on the government side but she was more Jacobite in her sympathies and when Cumberland's men found out that the Prince had been in Borrodale House, they tortured her to make her tell where he had gone. But by that time he was well away and she knew nothing anyway. They also arrested her husband and for a time it looked as if he would be executed in spite of his Hanoverian sympathies. He had to endure a year's imprisonment in Edinburgh Castle and was lucky to escape with his life. Their experiences poisoned Lady Macdonald's mind against Flora and she became her implacable enemy.

The people of Skye adored her ladyship, however. They even went so far as to rush out and pick stones out of her path as she rode by. Because she did not have a good word to say about Flora, the girl suffered from unpopularity on the island and many people suspected that she helped the Prince for selfish or pecuniary reasons. This unfair reputation stuck to her with some people for the rest of her life.

When she heard Lady Macdonald berating her daughter, Marion came hurrying down the long hall with her husband, the saturnine One-Eyed Hugh, following her. He was a sinister-looking fellow who wore a black patch over his missing eye and, because at one time he'd served as an officer in the French army, he behaved in a swaggering and disdainful fashion which always intimidated Flora. In his presence she reverted to being a frightened little girl because her mother had married him when she was only two years old.

Flora's father died young and her mother remarried within months. Marion claimed that Hugh abducted her against her will but gossips took that tale with a pinch of salt because she always appeared a very complaisant wife, leaving her two small children – Flora and her older brother – behind on Raasay, and going to live with her new husband at Armadale in Skye, rarely going back to see them. Flora's father's sisters, who brought the children up on the family estate at Milton on South Uist, always said that Marion was not the sort of woman to be abducted unless she wanted to go and they suspected she organized the whole thing in advance.

When Hugh saw Flora waiting in the hall, he barked out an order. 'Come on, girl, we must be on our way.' Flora literally jumped. She knew Marion was looking at her with a sceptical eye, obviously assessing her as a possible bride for Allan Macdonald.

The girl had fattened up a bit, her mother thought, and her skin was fine and pale but she was no great beauty. It was fortunate that she had such a good dowry or they might have had trouble marrying her off.

It always amazed Marion that her apparently timid daughter managed to acquit herself with such success when the Young Pretender was put into her care by Hugh. He hadn't wanted to take charge of the fugitive himself but was anxious to keep a foot in both camps so he gave the job to Flora, who he saw as expendable. Everyone had been astonished by the girl's resourcefulness, however, so there had to be more to her than there appeared even to her mother.

'Jump to it, girl, we must be on the road as soon as possible,' Hugh barked again in his grating voice and, as usual, Flora scuttled along behind him and Marion though all the time she was secretly thinking, 'When I get married to Allan Macdonald, at least I'll be free of you both and able to make my own decisions.'

No one seemed to have considered for a moment that she would turn down the marriage proposal and as they rode north she was informed that her wedding would be held at Armadale.

'When?' she asked, and Hugh turned in his saddle to tell her, 'In about a couple of weeks, I think. It'll only certainly go ahead after I arrange everything with his father.'

'What sort of things?' she persisted, amazed at her own daring. After all it was her life he was talking about.

'Money mostly. Old Macdonald's impressed by the amount you'll take to the match.'

'Do I have to give it all to my husband?' she wanted to know, and her mother chipped in, 'I doubt he'd be marrying you if you didn't. He's a good catch.'

And I'm not, thought Flora. She knew that her stepfather and the father of the groom, who was estate factor to the head of the Macdonald clan, were both shrewd businessmen, well aware of the purchasing power of her Jacobite dowry. She hoped that when the details of her marriage settlement were argued over, Hugh would have the strongest hand and that he would make sure that she would be housed in comfort when she married. Her experiences in London had made her yearn for better things than a basic bothy.

It was as if Hugh could read her mind. 'I'll make sure they don't put you into a bothy,' he told her, though he knew what the groom's father would say when the house stipulation was made. *'She was living in a bothy before you sent her out to take charge of the Prince.'*

It did not surprise him when, later, that was exactly what happened and during the discussions he leaned negligently back in his chair to say, 'Maybe she was living in a bothy then but she's seen a lot and done a lot since. Your son is marrying a famous woman – with money. If he applies himself, they could live very comfortably on what she brings him.'

When he stressed the word *if*, the groom's father dropped his eyes and said, 'My son will do very well by her, you can be sure of that.' They both knew that Allan was none too keen on sustained hard work.

In the end, after days of discussion at Armadale, a five-page wedding contract was drawn up and presented to the young couple for them to sign. It was very precise and stated that Flora was to retain the sum of £50 for herself but the rest of her money was to be given into the hands of her husband who, hopefully, would use it to earn a profit with which to provide a comfortable life for her and any children born to them.

At Hugh's insistence it also stated that she was to live in a comfortable house that was suitable for someone of her gentlewoman status.

There was no time for courting or getting to know each other. Allan was working on another part of the estate and Flora was kept busy in Armadale House by her mother who supervised the making of her trousseau and the filling of her linen chest.

It took several weeks before the details of the marriage contract were decided, and at last the lawyer called in the young couple to sign the contract. Allan, who looked to Flora as handsome as a god, wrote his name fluently with a curling dash beneath it because he had received his education in Edinburgh at the Royal High School, but when she took up the pen to sign her name she was thankful that she had taken the trouble to attend Mr Beatt's writing classes in Edinburgh after she was released from prison in England.

Before she went south she had been scantily educated and was barely able to write except in childish capitals. Even after studying at Mr Beatt's she still found writing more than a few words difficult but when she stood back to look at what she had written on her marriage contract she thought her signature looked quite impressive.

FLORA MACDONALD . . . She'd taken care to make sure her signature was large and that her first name stood out proudly because it irked her that in the contract, she was referred to throughout as Florrie, which made her feel diminished and unimportant.

She did not want to revert to her previous lowly standing. Now she was the Flora Macdonald who had mixed with the gentry and sat to have her flattering portrait painted in Edinburgh. Her full name made her feel proud. 'I'm Flora now, not Florrie the tender of sheep and cattle,' she thought with some pride.

On the morning of her wedding day on November 6th, the weather was kind and a late autumn sun beamed down from a cloudless sky. The sea was a deep shade of aquamarine that made a startling contrast with the purple heather-covered slopes of the surrounding mountains.

'Happy is the bride the sun shines on,' said Chrissie as she dressed

Flora in the Royal Stewart tartan gown that she'd worn when she was painted by Alan Ramsay. It was made of the finest silk and had been a gift from Lady Primrose.

Flora's hands were shaking and her heart beating fast because she was in a state of confusion, asking herself if she was doing the right thing by marrying the handsome Allan Macdonald, the factor's son, who she admired but barely knew.

He moved socially in another world and it never struck her that she would be the woman he chose as his wife. The old Florrie Macdonald was a nobody with no status and no money, and, she was honest enough to admit, no great beauty, though Chrissie always praised the frankness of her face and big blue eyes. Without being aware of it, she also had a fund of calm charm which beguiled people when they took the trouble to really talk to her. That was what ensured good treatment for her when she was a prisoner of the English.

While Chrissie was dressing her hair on the wedding morning, she suddenly said, 'I hope he is not marrying me because his father has told him to or because he wants my dowry.'

Chrissie put down the comb and glared into the little spotted mirror. 'He's a lucky man to be getting you and I'm sure he knows it,' she said.

'But I'm so ignorant.'

'He went to a good school but that doesn't mean anything when you're making your way through life,' said Chrissie.

'I mean I'm ignorant about what happens between a man and a woman when they're married. I know about animals, of course, but I don't know how to please a man.' Flora sounded anguished.

'It's up to him to please you,' Chrissie told her. She knew that people gossiped and said Flora had fallen in love and slept with Prince Charlie but she guessed that was untrue.

Marion had been the only person bold enough to raise the subject with her daughter. 'Did you share the Prince's bed?' she asked Flora one day when the marriage negotiations were going on and Flora had been genuinely horrified.

'Of course not!' she said.

In fact she realized that the very idea repelled her. There was something about Charles Edward Stuart that made her withdraw from him even when he was turning on the full force of his considerable charm. To do him justice he had never attempted to seduce her either.

But during the last few weeks she was surprised by how strongly she was attracted to Allan Macdonald and the more she saw of him the more unworthy she felt to be marrying him. Even if he was marrying her for financial reasons, she told herself, she could only hope that one day they would feel genuine love for each other.

Chrissie was having none of that. 'You're the best bride he could get in the whole of the Islands, and I'm sure he knows it,' she said firmly, gently laying a coronet of curled tartan ribbons on Flora's head.

Both Allan and Flora were Protestants so they were married by a black-clad preacher in Armadale, her stepfather's big house. As she walked across the room to stand beside her new husband she was overwhelmed again by his handsomeness.

Chrissie was right; he was a fine-looking man. He stood beside her, tall and straight with his jet-black hair tied back in a queue, and his strong-featured face looking set, stern and serious. In spite of the recently imposed English laws against the wearing of tartan, he had a brightly coloured Macdonald plaid draped over one shoulder. It was both an act of Jacobite defiance and a compliment to his new wife.

She stepped up to his side and smiled up at him. His expression softened and he reached out to hold her hand while she took her vows. His hand completely covered hers and she let it lie in his palm, feeling that she had come home to a safe haven.

When she took her vows and became his wife, her voice was strong and confident. She firmly resolved to help him as much as she possibly could for as long as they both lived.

One-Eyed Hugh loved a good party and he led the revels after Flora's wedding. Holding both hands above his head he danced to the music of the band of fiddlers who crowded together at the end of his big hall. His voice rang out over the music as he called out to the bride and groom, 'Get up and dance. Show us how you move together! If you can't dance you can't fuck!'

Then he caught his giggling wife Marion round the waist and whirled her off into the middle of the floor. As Flora watched her mother, she knew for certain that Marion's story about being abducted against her will was a fabrication. There was a chemistry between her mother and her stepfather that seemed to throb in the room and she looked shyly at her new husband wondering what lay ahead for her – would there be sexual magnetism between them, too?

She was a reticent girl, who hid her feelings and tried to deny even to herself that she had any romantic feelings, perhaps because she was used to hearing people gossip about her mother, but now she hoped that some of Marion's reputed red-bloodedness had been passed down to her.

She wondered if her new husband had heard the speculations about herself and the Prince but he did not seem to have any doubts about her. With a loud laugh at Hugh's antics, he took Flora's hand and drew her on to the floor and, yes, he could dance very well. *That's a good sign*, she thought, and felt herself blush at the idea.

At midnight, when all the men and some of the women were happily intoxicated on Hugh's good claret, a posse of people bore down on Flora and Allan and manhandled them upstairs, putting them to bed in Marion and Hugh's big chamber.

Marion slipped a length of ribbon round Flora's neck when she tucked her under the quilt and, as she pulled the curtains tight, Hugh yelled, 'Go to it!'

Then they all went out, slamming the bedroom door behind them. For the next half-hour the newly married pair lay still, not even touching each other while they were serenaded by catcalls and the banging of cooking pots beneath their window, but eventually the revellers tired and went back to drinking and dancing.

Unfortunately Allan was as drunk as everyone else at the revels and he fell asleep with one arm flung over Flora and his bright plaid spread out over them both. She lay awake for a while but eventually slipped into the sleep of exhaustion. 'Am I too unappealing for him to stay awake long enough to make love to me?' she wondered sadly.

She wakened as the first streaks of pale dawn striped the sky outside their window and found Allan eager to consummate their marriage in energetic style. 'I could learn to enjoy this,' she thought as she lay back against the pillows after the third time.

When she saw her mother later in the morning, the first thing Marion did was slip the same length of ribbon round her neck and then cry out to Allan, 'Well done. You've done her proud. And I can tell you've planted a seed in her last night as well. My first grandchild'll be born next summer.'

'How do you know that?' Flora asked.

'A woman's neck swells when she loses her virginity,' said Marion, 'and I can always tell by her eyes if a woman is pregnant.'

She was right about both things.

Most of the wedding guests were still drunk at noon so it was not till after more hours of carousing that a bleary-eyed Allan took his bride away to her new home. Flora rode pillion on her new husband's horse and Hugh and Marion went with them.

When Flora saw what was to be her home, her heart sank and she gave a wry smile when she remembered the style in which she had lived with Lady Primrose – or even where she lodged as a prisoner in the Tower of London.

Her new home had an earth floor and a sagging roof thatched with heather. The furniture was rough and basic and there were only two rooms, with a byre for animals tacked on to the kitchen.

Hugh saw her dismay and said roughly, 'It's the best I could get out of your father-in-law but he can't live forever and when he goes Allan'll be the next factor and you'll get the factor's house. Make the best of it for now, girl.'

She made the best of it. There was no alternative and after time she forgot about elegant rooms and fine furniture as she tended her string of infants, dragged buckets of water from their well or bent to cook broth over a reeking peat fire.

The Flora Macdonald who'd posed in Royal Stewart tartan for Alan Ramsay became the wife of the factor's son. None of her neighbours liked her because they thought she gave herself airs and also because they said she had profited from helping the Prince to escape the redcoats while so many of them had suffered.

The dowry Lady Primrose collected for her from the Jacobite ladies of London was held against her in Skye for the rest of her life.

Five

'I can't understand you! What has happened to you?' Catherine Walkinshaw was very irritated by her youngest sister who alternated between moods of deepest depression followed by what seemed like hysterical joy.

Clementine turned on her heel and stared over her shoulder, eyes wide in surprise. 'Nothing's wrong with me. I've been making up my mind what to do with my life and I've decided to become a nun.'

'A *nun*!' Catherine was thunderstruck.

Clementine nodded. 'Yes, at Douai. It's a convent only for highborn ladies. You have to prove your ancestry before they accept you.'

Catherine had to sit down in order to absorb this idea. 'In Douai. The Low Countries. But you're not a Roman Catholic . . .'

'Of course I am. I converted years ago.'

'But the rest of the family are Protestants. I thought you'd given all that Catholic thing up long ago.' Catherine was genuinely shocked.

'You can't give up a belief like mine.'

Clementine sounded so determined that her sister knew there was no point arguing so she pulled a face and asked, 'How has all this come about? Has it something to do with that Irishman O'Sullivan coming here to see you after Lady Primrose's party? I didn't want to let him in. I wish I hadn't. He's dangerous. He was one of the seven men of Moidart who met the Young Pretender when he first landed in Scotland, wasn't he? I don't like any of us to be associated with people like him. Don't you realize it could cost me my position?' Catherine was working herself up and shaking with rage.

Clementine was still unrepentant. 'Don't be silly. Your mistress's husband the Prince of Wales went to meet Prince Charlie when he was at Lady Primrose's because he hates his father and his brother Cumberland. He might even try to help Charles get back to Scotland if it was to do his father and his butcher brother down. You know that as well as I do.'

'Mind your tongue, for God's sake. Talking like that is treason. What Prince Frederick thinks is his business and he would never contemplate backing another Jacobite rebellion. He has more sense.'

'Sense! None of those Hanoverians has any sense. They're as stupid as donkeys. You only support them because they provide your bread and butter and give you a place at court!'

Catherine ran across the room and seized her sister by the shoulders. 'The sooner you go to Douai the better and good riddance. The nuns are welcome to you because no one else will have you.'

Clementine threw back her head and gave a strange laugh. 'You'll eat your words, sister,' she said.

That night she left her sister's rooms in St James' Palace and took herself back to Scotland, to her uncle's house at Bannockburn where her mother was living. There she waited and brooded, her moods continuing to change as swiftly as the weather. Her state of mind seemed to depend on the letters that arrived for her from time to time.

Six months passed, during which she grew thinner and more distracted. Her mother, in despair, said to her eldest daughter Barbara, 'Sometimes I fear for Clemmie's mind.'

'She's never been normal, not since she fell in love with the Prince. That was the undoing of her,' said Barbara dismissively.

Her mother nodded and said, 'I wish that man's foot had never crossed this threshold. Clemmie's talking of joining a Papist nunnery and I'm afraid that it's probably the best place for her.'

'She's spending all her money in order to get them to accept her. It's a very exclusive place apparently and she has to pay a big dowry to get in as well as prove she's not base born.'

'She's certainly not base born. I'm the sister of a peer and her father came from a good family even though he made his fortune in trade,' said her mother defensively.

'The Douai nuns are all very high born but it seems as if they'll take her now. She must have persuaded someone to advocate her case. I wonder who it was?' said Barbara, who was under no misapprehensions about her background.

'Whoever it is I hope they get her to Douai before she drives me mad with her switching between weeping and wailing and acting as if she's found a treasure trove,' said the girls' mother fretfully.

Their conversation was interrupted by the hurried arrival of an exhilarated Clementine who rushed up to her mother and took her hands, saying, 'I've just heard that all the arrangements for Douai have been made. I leave in two days' time. I hope I have your blessing, Mother dear.'

The old woman stared at her youngest child with tears rising in her eyes. Clemmie had always been a sweet-natured girl but somehow nothing ever seemed to go right for her and her involvement with Charles Edward Stewart had almost broken her spirit.

Now however it looked as if her hopes of happiness were rising again. Perhaps a life of piety in a convent would suit her because there had been no sign of her making a marriage.

'Clemmie dearest, are you sure that you are doing the right thing? Is your religious faith strong enough to spend the rest of your life in a convent? And with you so far away, I'll probably never see you again,' she said piteously.

Clementine knelt at her mother's feet and told her, 'I will write to you and I promise that I'll be happy where I am going. Happier than I have ever been before.'

'Does that mean you've had some kind of revelation?' asked Barbara caustically.

Clementine smiled beatifically. 'Indeed it does.'

'How are you getting to Douai? You can't travel without some protection,' said their mother.

'Colonel O'Sullivan has offered to escort me.'

'O'Sullivan. One of Charlie's men who was here with him when he was ill? How is he involved?' Barbara wanted to know.

'He corresponds with me from time to time and has helped me arrange my acceptance at Douai. He's a staunch Roman Catholic and knows the abbess there.'

Her mother gave a moan. 'Oh, I wish I'd had some sons instead of only daughters. If you'd had a brother, he wouldn't let you go off to Flanders alone with a stranger – and to join a nunnery.'

'If she had a brother, he'd probably stop her going anywhere by locking her up. Don't worry, Mother, she'll probably be back within six months,' snapped Barbara who thought the whole expedition highly suspect.

She was not the only one. When Colonel O'Sullivan arrived to take Clementine away he was distinctly down in the mouth and spent his time complaining about the bad sea crossing he had just endured. In fact his real complaint was that he had been ordered by the Prince to deliver Miss Walkinshaw to Flanders after Charles had tried and failed to persuade his secretary Goring to undertake the task – Goring refused to have anything to do with it. He even went so far as to write to Charles' brother Henry, the Cardinal of York in Rome, and tell him about this latest whim of his brother.

'He is living in Paris but is set on bringing a low-born young woman from Scotland to be his mistress. I am afraid that he is building up trouble for himself because her sister is Lady of the Bedchamber to the wife of the Prince of Wales and it is possible that she might be planted as a spy in your brother's household,' Goring wrote, planting the seeds of deep suspicion of Clementine that was to be her undoing with Charles' family and their supporters.

On receipt of this letter, both Henry and his agitated father wrote furious letters to Charles on the subject but that only made him more determined to import Clementine as his mistress. He could never bring himself to do anything his father wanted.

'I am at a very low ebb in my spirits and what I need is the company of someone who truly loves me,' he wrote to Clementine, urging her to join him.

She treasured his letter, and read it over and over again till the paper was so crinkled and the ink so faded that it was almost illegible. She then kept it folded up tightly and tucked into her bodice next to her heart.

The parting with her family was tearful and she found it difficult to hide the real reason for her voyage to Douai from her mother and sisters because she was afraid that they would take steps to forcibly prevent her going if they knew the truth.

The sea passage was as stormy as O'Sullivan feared but, though Clementine was horribly sick, her spirits remained high because she believed she was soon to see the man she adored.

Six

'Who exactly is she?' one scornful-looking nun asked her companion as they walked past the chapel and saw a huddled figure kneeling before the altar with her head supported on her cupped hands.

'I've no idea but she has no style and nothing of any quality with her. The abbess is being very tight-lipped about the whole thing. I think she's been asked to hide her by someone important,' was the reply.

The first nun laughed. 'I doubt if she's a princess in hiding. She looks more like a dairy maid.'

They walked on, robes rustling, not caring that Clementine might have heard them, which in fact was the case.

She bent her head even lower and tried to pray. Her strong Roman Catholic religious faith had strengthened even more since she left England, and now, in a desperate state of anxiety, she was seeking help from God.

'Where is he? Why was he not in Douai to meet me? He knew I was coming here. He asked me to come!' The words ran through her mind again and again, but she never received any answers.

She had been in the convent for three weeks and was totally overwhelmed by the grandeur of the place and the snobbery of the nuns who lived there. They were all from the best families of Europe, women whose black habits were made of silk and who kept their pet dogs, their horses, musicians and retinues of servants though they had ostensibly taken the veil. Douai was the most exclusive convent since Fontevrault in France gave refuge to Eleanor of Aquitaine, who went to live there after leaving her husband, King Henry II of England, some six hundred years before.

Clementine raised her eyes and fixed them on a magnificent carving of Christ on the Cross that hung directly in front of her. 'Help me,' she pleaded. 'Please help me.'

She was painfully aware that she had burned her boats by

leaving her home and family and setting out on what was a massive deception, for she had told her mother and sisters she was planning to become a deaconess of this convent. Nothing was farther from the truth and in fact the abbess made it clear from the moment she crossed the threshold that the sooner she was off the premises the better.

But Prince Charles, who organized the whole thing and summoned her there, seemed to have forgotten all about her. Colonel O'Sullivan, who had been her escort on the journey from Scotland, had also disappeared and she had not seen or heard from him since the night of her arrival.

She was desperate but there was no one to whom she could turn for advice. 'What am I to do? Have I been deceived? Did I misunderstand what the Prince required of me?' she asked the crucified Christ but there was no reply and hot tears ran down her cheeks.

Over and over again she told herself that there had to be some genuine reason for Charles not appearing to rescue her. She remembered his wonderfully caring letters which swore eternal love to her. 'You must come to me because no one in the world is more fitted to soothe my sorrows than you,' he'd written, and she believed every word. It never occurred to her that his pleas were always selfish and there was never a word about how much he loved her.

She was besotted and her whole existence was centred on him. If he did not come soon, she was sure she would die of grief.

As she was beginning to sob again, she felt a hand on her shoulder and a lay sister said in guttural broken English, 'Come. You must come. A messenger awaits you.'

Clementine sprang to her feet, suddenly enlivened. 'A messenger? Is it my Prince? Is it the Young Chevalier?'

'Old Chevalier,' said the woman who was one of the older and friendlier members of the convent and the only nun who did not look down her nose when she passed Clementine in the corridors.

'His father? Surely you don't mean his father?' asked Clementine, horrified.

The old woman shrugged uncomprehendingly and crooked her finger. 'Come, come . . .' She led the way to a reception room beside the main gate of the convent where a tall figure in black stood leaning one arm on the mantelshelf and staring down into the burning coals.

'Colonel O'Sullivan!' cried Clementine, half in relief and half in disappointment. It was not the man she wanted to see but at least it was one who she recognized.

He seemed more ill at ease than usual but he had never been relaxed with her. 'Ah, Miss Walkinshaw, I hope you are rested after your travels. I'm sure the nuns will have looked after you well.'

She brushed aside his niceties with a gesture of the hand. 'Oh very well, and I have had many weeks to recover. But where is my Prince?'

O'Sullivan smiled but still looked shifty. 'He's asked me to convey you to Paris.'

'To Paris? Why didn't he come to see me himself? Is he ill? Why has he been detained in Paris?'

'He is quite well but he would like you to meet him in Paris. It's a beautiful city and he has acquired fine lodgings there.' O'Sullivan shuffled his feet because he was obviously not enjoying this assignment, but at the mention of fine lodgings she clasped her hands in delight, imagining Charles waiting for her in some sumptuous palace with his arms open to embrace her.

He is being romantic because Paris is the perfect place for lovers to re-unite, she told herself.

'Will it take us long to get to Paris?' she asked O'Sullivan, for she was not sure of the geographical location of Douai.

O'Sullivan assumed what he hoped was a reassuring smile. 'It's not too far away. It will only take us a few days,' he said.

'How many?' she asked suspiciously.

'About three in a fast conveyance. It is about a hundred and twenty miles, you see.'

Something about his manner made her stiffen. 'And the Prince will be waiting for me there, will he?' she asked.

'Oh yes. He was quite specific that I should take you to Paris. He's taken a suite of rooms.' O'Sullivan had no idea what Charles intended to do with the woman after she was delivered to Paris. His job was only to get her there.

'A suite of rooms? Is he there now?' Obviously it was no

princely palace. She was bemused and struggled to take in all this information.

In fact O'Sullivan knew that Charles was only forty miles away in Ghent but he had been ordered to take this woman to Paris and there was no alternative but do as he was told, though he felt pity for the poor plain lass, who, he was sure, had no idea what she was getting into. It appeared that Charles' intention was to make her a common mistress and award her no position of respect.

His master's capricious behaviour since he escaped from Scotland was getting on O'Sullivan's nerves but he was a loyal Jacobite, who had been one of the loyal Irish supporters to accompany the Young Chevalier when he'd landed at Moidart in 1745. Though often provoked, he would not give up his allegiance lightly.

It had been arranged that he and Miss Walkinshaw should travel to Paris under assumed names, and so it was as Monsieur and Madame Jackson that they made the long and tedious journey from Douai. As they covered the miles, a desperately worried Clementine poured out her anxieties to her escort who listened and did his best to soothe them, though he felt he was lying to no purpose. What he should have said to the poor woman was that he felt she was making a terrible mistake and would never be considered a respectable woman again.

'I wish I could let my mother know where I am because she and my sisters think I'm still at Douai,' she said sadly on the last morning of their journey.

'Didn't you tell them about your arrangement with the Prince when you left?' O'Sullivan asked.

'No, they believed I was about to become a postulant at Douai. When I am finally settled with the Prince I'll write to them and explain that it was love that took me away from them. Then they'll understand what made me lie. If they'd known I was taking off into the unknown and that my Prince wouldn't even be at Douai to meet me, they would have done everything in their power to stop me going. They'd probably have had me locked up!' she told him.

He nodded, silently agreeing with them and not knowing what to say to her.

'But when I am able to write and tell them that I am about

to be married, they'll be very pleased and forgive me. They're all Jacobites at heart, you see,' said Clementine, looking into his face and anxiously trying to read his expression.

O'Sullivan inwardly groaned and kept his face impassive and his feelings hidden, for he very much doubted that Charles had any intention of marrying this girl. During their acquaintance, there had been several mistresses following in Charles' train and when some woman caught the Prince's attention, there was usually a short honeymoon period before his initial fervour wore off – which it always did.

In this girl's case, however, the Prince was behaving strangely. It seemed that once he had talked her into running away to him, he'd lost enthusiasm even before the affair began and kept putting off meeting her for as long as possible. If O'Sullivan had not continually reminded him about the woman waiting in the convent, he might have left her there for ever.

Women did not come very high in the Prince's list of necessities for a happy life. Brandy, compliments and luxurious living, as well as baiting his brother Henry and antagonizing his father, were far higher up that list.

When they reached the crowded streets of Paris, Clementine stared out of the carriage window at the sights, sounds and smells of the city and gasped in admiration. She exclaimed at every fine building they approached, obviously expecting to draw up before one of them, but they kept driving on until they finally came to a stop in front of a very ordinary-looking lodging house and she looked round at her escort in dismay as she asked, 'Are we stopping *here*?' The place looked so unprepossessing that she could not believe a Prince would even want to step over the threshold. The Walkinshaw family had been in trade, it was true, but they were rich and used to better accommodation than this.

'Our Prince is living in disguise. He doesn't want his father to know what he's doing. There are spies watching him all the time because the King of France plays one side against the other, you see. He doesn't want to antagonize the English too much at the moment,' said O'Sullivan hurriedly.

'But it was the French who rescued the Prince from Scotland. They were on his side against the English then,' protested Clementine.

'Things change quickly in diplomacy,' said O'Sullivan guardedly. He knew that since the signing of the treaty of Aix between France and England, the French king did not want to have anything openly to do with Charles, and regarded him as an embarrassment.

Also he was greatly antagonized by the way the young Stewart flaunted himself around and talked grandly of launching another expedition to regain his rightful kingdom, as he called it. Louis had no intention at all of having anything to do with that again.

Charles was so persistent however that he had eventually been ordered by the King to leave Paris, but he refused to go and continued to flaunt himself at the Opera and in the cafés of the Bois de Boulogne till, in an embarrassing incident, he was finally arrested and tied up like an angry chicken with black tape before being sent in exile to Avignon.

'Stay there and don't come back!' he was told but paid no heed and returned to Paris under a false name and continued to be a perpetual embarrassment to the French king.

Clementine knew nothing of this and when she alighted from her carriage in front of the lodging house, she did not know that her lackadaisical lover, currently masquerading as Chevalier William Johnson, was not there waiting for her but hiding in another convent nearby in the Rue Domenique. Devastated when she found that he was not at the lodging house waiting to greet her, she took to her bed and was lying desolate and weeping when there was a scuffle at the door and it was thrown open finally to reveal the Prince on the threshold.

He looked magnificent in satin breeches and a richly embroidered coat and waistcoat. She sat bolt upright to stare at him, as if she was unable to bear the glory of the sight.

'Oh, my dearest Prince!' she cried, jumping off the bed and throwing herself at him. Beaming because he loved being loved and enjoyed acting the part of the adored hero, he spread out his arms to embrace her and hold her close, whispering her name over and over. 'Clementina!'

All her doubts and misgivings disappeared. She laid her cheek against his chest and listened to the beating of his heart. 'I love you, oh, how I love you,' she sobbed. Now she knew that she had done the right thing by running away from her home and family to join him, for this was the man she loved and would love till she died.

'Oh my dearest heart,' she sobbed, 'I love you, how I love you. I'll serve you forever.' Because she buried her face in the front of his richly embroidered waistcoat, she failed to smell the brandy on his breath until he held her face between his palms and stared into her eyes.

He was equally moved by their reunion and delighted by her reception of him. 'This is the sort of woman I've always wanted. She'll obey my every whim and never find a fault with me,' he thought. With her there would be no screaming rows like he'd endured with that opera singer and other demanding women. He'd made a good choice by bringing her here. He needed to have a woman around and the emotional part of his life had been empty since his mother abandoned him to take up religion. This adoring Clementina would fill the gap but make no demands on him.

'My dearest heart,' he whispered and kissed her on the lips but got no erotic thrill from doing so.

He had disappointing news for her, however. Because of the disapproval of the King, he was not going to be able to stay for long in beautiful, exciting Paris. After only one night together, he told her, 'Now I must leave this city.'

'Where are we going?' she asked.

'I'm going to Ghent. But I must go alone at first to take a house there that will make the perfect home for the two of us. Then you can follow me. Stay here for the meantime and I'll let you know when the house will be ready for you,' he told her.

She was confused and asked anxiously, 'But I know no one here. Why can't I come with you now?'

He shook his head firmly. 'I've told you what you must do. O'Sullivan will be here and he'll bring you on later,' he said. She was not to know that he hated to stay anywhere for long and that their strange life of comings and goings and perpetual unexplained separations was only just beginning.

He was never able to endure spending long periods of time with one person, especially one woman, and he hated other people's need for wanting to know about his comings and goings. His compulsion to flit about at will was almost paranoid.

'I do not want to stay here alone. I don't even know where you are going. Please take me with you,' she pleaded, not realizing she was verging on dangerous ground.

He was adjusting his wig but he whirled round and glared at her. 'Don't you realize there are spies around me all the time? I have many enemies and too many prying eyes are watching me. They might even try to kill me! You must follow later. O'Sullivan's been a good escort so far, hasn't he?'

'Oh yes, but he's not you and it's you I came here to be with. It's for you that I left my home and family.'

He snapped, 'That was your decision. Now do as I say for I have my reasons.' But as soon as he spoke, his bad temper seemed to disappear and he walked across to the bed to kiss her fondly and caress her breasts. Reassured, she gave herself up to him like a purring cat.

He was right about the number of spies who surrounded him. Nothing he did went unreported either to the King of France or to his father and brother in Rome and usually to them all.

James was furious when news reached him that his son had taken up with another woman, and one who was reputed to have connections in the Hanoverian court for her sister was Lady of the Bedchamber to the Princess of Wales.

'He's gone mad. He's sleeping with a Hanoverian spy!' exclaimed the Old Pretender.

For years he had been sending his son angry – and always unanswered – letters pleading with him to behave himself more decorously, live more frugally and stop boasting about being about to start a third rising in Scotland.

'I didn't want you to go there in the first place,' wrote James and warned his son that if he kept on antagonizing the King of France, he would find himself in penury.

Charles refused to accept his father's advice, and went on talking openly about regaining the rightful throne of England, Scotland, Ireland and Wales for the Stewarts. Unaware how close he was treading to disaster, he pestered the shrewd Louis XV of France to lend him money, ships and men for his next expedition.

'You will not regret backing me,' he wrote. 'Remember that I had the English running like rabets the last time I fought against them.'

Louis threw the letter away but spies sent a copy of it to Charles' father who read it out to his youngest son Cardinal Henry and both shook their heads in despair. 'I'm afraid your brother is an unteachable halfwit and always has been. When he was small I thought he might even turn out to be a lunatic because he found it so hard to learn anything. And he is still learning nothing from his past mistakes,' James said sadly.

Henry agreed and wished fervently that Charles could emerge from his cloud cuckoo land. It was shaming to the Cardinal that his brother so blithely found it convenient to forget the debacle of Culloden. Instead of being ashamed, Charles still went about Europe boasting about the rigours he suffered when escaping from Scotland, telling anyone who would listen how he'd marched for miles across heather-covered hills in rags and broken shoes. The more he told the story, the more he came to believe his tales of his own heroic achievements.

Clementine was left fretting in Paris for two weeks until her faith in Charles was again fortified. In early June he wrote to tell her that he had found 'a pretti house with a room in it for a friend' in Ghent. She was to go there at once.

Their happiest time together began then, and they set up home together in the 'pretti' house which became a place of such happiness and peace that the long-suffering members of Charles' entourage began to relax and think that their employer had at last reached a state of tranquillity.

The loving couple conducted themselves modestly in Ghent, promenading in the warm evenings arm in arm and making music together on rainy days. He was a very good musician and she played the viol competently as well as singing in a sweet treble voice.

No longer did he drink himself insensible every night. No longer did he throw terrifying fits of temper at the least little irritation. He even read the letters from his father without tearing them into tiny pieces and scattering them all over the floor – but they still went unanswered.

Everyone was surprised by the change that came over him. 'The new woman is really changing him. Perhaps he'll settle down at last and become more mature,' said O'Sullivan to the Prince's secretary.

Goring, however, looked doubtful and said, 'I agree he is more settled but will it last? Let's hope so.'

The letters from Rome were the only thing that disrupted the domestic harmony. The Old Pretender poured out screeds of advice to his son, all of which were ignored. The admonitions about spending too much money were what most angered Charles.

'How dare he tell me that I must economize! He lives like a hermit. He has no idea of keeping up the grandeur of his position. No wonder my mother left him. She could not abide his cheese paring,' Charles told Clementine after every letter, but he was not so violent against his father as he would have been before she moved in with him.

'But we live very modestly,' she said, agreeing with him.

He nodded. 'Indeed we do. With my status in life I should be housed in a palace like Versailles. My father doesn't realize that I'm the one who should be complaining. He refuses to finance another expedition to Scotland. He will absolutely not hear of it. "Let it be", he says, but he is an old man, too tired to go campaigning and yet he won't let me go on his behalf. I'm a young man who wants to re-establish my family in its rightful place. Those Germans in London should be thrown out on their ears.'

Clementine laid her hand on his arm and stroked it softly. 'If you were to land again in Scotland, the people would flock to you,' she assured him.

'I know it. My brother knows it too but he's jealous of me; he's always been jealous. That's why he clings to my father as he does and influences his mind. He won't go campaigning, not him. He's a pederast who likes to be surrounded by lisping young men. He had a favourite that our father made him give up, but now he has another that he says is his secretary. He's afraid of the old man so he lives a lie. I can't do that.'

Clementine clicked her tongue in disapproval of Henry but said nothing because she was sufficiently realistic to know that it was in both her and Charles' interests not to antagonize his brother too much for he controlled the father and the father controlled the purse strings.

In fact, taking her courage in both hands, Clementine secretly wrote to Henry, telling him that she was taking care of his brother and would do nothing to compromise him. This letter received a courteous though guarded reply but Henry was pleased because lines of communication between Charles and Rome were now being gently opened by his new mistress.

Letters were as big a source of anxiety to her as they were to the Prince because as soon as she was settled in the house in Ghent, she wrote to her mother and sisters, giving her address and telling them that she was living unmarried with the Young Chevalier. She knew that this unconventional situation offended their Scottish morality but she assured her family that she loved him and he loved her.

The only reply she received was from her sister Catherine in London who berated her roundly for deceitfulness and immorality. How could she so demean herself as to live with a drunken sot as his common whore? Catherine added that their mother was grief stricken and never wanted to see her youngest daughter again. 'As far as our mother is concerned, you have ceased to exist,' Catherine wrote.

Clementine wept over that and wrote several times more but never received another reply. She took care to hide her unhappiness from Charles because he did not like to see her cast down, and anyway, whenever she was in his company her delight was so overwhelming that she forgot her other woes.

In late May of 1753, one of Charles' Dutch supporters commissioned a young Ghent artist to paint the Prince's portrait so that copies of it could be distributed among the Jacobite following. Charles liked being painted, and wanted to strike a histrionic pose staring ahead like the victor of a battle. This artist disagreed, however, and wanted to paint him sitting looking reflective with a Stewart tartan plaid draped over one shoulder.

Sitting quietly for hours at a time did not suit Charles' temperament and the chosen painter worked so slowly that his patience soon ran out.

One morning, when she saw he was fidgeting worse than ever for the day was warm, Clementine brought in a tankard of chilled wine to soothe his temper. It worked for a little while but it sharpened his longing for alcohol, which he had avoided for some time, and when the first tankard was emptied he demanded another, which she obligingly fetched for him.

He drank that down quickly and soon wanted another and another. Unfortunately, with each tankard that he drank he became more and more abusive of the painter, and also of Clementine and everyone else around him. It took two days, and the ingestion of several bottles of wine, before the portrait was finished.

On the last day the artist put down his brush, wiped his fingers on an oiled rag and said, 'It is done, sire.'

Charles was slumped inelegantly in his chair with the plaid twisted round his waist. He was very drunk and looked caustic when the artist proudly stood back to survey his work. Clementine ran across the floor too and smiled at the anxious young man when she looked at it. She was determined to be complimentary to make up for Charles' surliness.

'It's magnificent,' she exclaimed. 'You've caught a masterly likeness.'

The sitter then staggered up from his seat and came across to stand beside them, staying silent for a long time while he stared at the still-wet canvas. Then he suddenly reached out his right hand and deliberately smeared out the features of the painted face. Viciously he rubbed and rubbed until the artist's work was unrecognizable. The portrait was ruined.

'You're not a painter, you're a charlatan,' he snapped to the horrified young man who saw days of work disappearing before his eyes. His commission was up in smoke.

'But I think it was very good, and very like you,' Clementine protested.

Charles turned on her too. 'Oh, do you? You're a fool. What do you know of painting?' To the cowering painter he shouted, 'Get out of here and take your daub with you.'

As the young man started to hurry away, loaded down with pots and brushes, in sympathy Clementine got up to help him but Charles snapped, 'Sit down, woman. Let him go.'

His face was red and furious but she had no idea what had made him so angry for, as far as she could see, the portrait was actually very like him and competently painted.

As soon as the door was closed behind the artist, and they were alone, she tried to soothe Charles by saying, 'Have some more wine and don't be so angry. It was quite good work.'

She went across to the corner where the wine was waiting,

and as she was filling a tankard, she went on, 'What upset you so much about the picture, my dearest one?'

He ran across the floor in a fury and seized her upper arm in a cruel grip. 'Upset me? That man painted me and made me look as if I was a drunken old man. Did you see the way he plumped up my cheeks and chin? Did you see the colour he made my face – it was puce I tell you, puce!'

She drew her arm back from him, terrified by his violence. In fact his face *was* puce and, if she was to be honest, it had been puce for days. His cheeks were full and there was a heavy swelling beneath his chin. Bonnie Prince Charlie was not bonny any longer and it was the first time she had really noticed the change that had come over him.

Furious at the realization he saw in her eyes, he began shaking her to and fro, pulling her off her feet and throwing her on to the ground. When she saw him lift his foot to kick her she cried out, 'Spare me, my lord, spare me. I am carrying your child. Please do not hurt it.'

He stopped in mid kick and stared down at her. 'You are carrying a child? It is mine?'

She crawled on to her knees and clung to his legs, 'Of course it's yours. It should be born in the autumn, in October I think.'

He changed at once, hauled her up and hugged her tight. 'Oh my dearest, you have made me a very happy man.' But he did not apologize for being about to beat her. Perhaps princes need not apologize for things like that, she thought – and so did he.

It seemed he wanted to parade her more and more in public as she grew heavily pregnant. It was as if he was using her big belly to convince the world that he was capable of procreation. When she was carrying her child proudly before her, he announced that they were to leave the backwater of Ghent and take a house in Liège, which was nearer to Paris, the centre of civilization.

Their new establishment was much grander than the little house in Ghent and when they moved in they now did so under the names of Count and Countess Johnson. Charles was moving them up the social scale and when she asked why he did not use his real name he was horrified. He liked his life of subterfuge.

It made him feel important even though he knew that no one of any importance was deceived.

His insistence that part of his secrecy was due to a fear of assassination scared Clementine but she found it puzzling that even when he was pretending to be someone else, he certainly did not hide away but lived in great style and swaggered around in Liège society, dressed in the most magnificent clothes and behaving like an anointed king.

He also began disappearing for days on end without telling her where he was going, but when he was at home, he took a great interest in the progress of her pregnancy and was touchingly attentive.

Her labour began in the early hours of a fine October day and lasted for twelve hours. While she lay writhing and groaning in bed, she heard him striding up and down the passage outside their bedroom. At last she gave a great push and the baby came into the world. As she lay back against her pillows she heard the midwife cry, 'It's a girl.'

When she woke a few hours later he was sitting by the bed. 'I'm sorry,' she said. 'I know you wanted a boy.'

'Not at all, you've given me a lovely daughter and I will call her Charlotte,' he said and took her hand.

She fell asleep again thinking that because Charlotte was the female version of his own name, it meant he'd accepted her.

While she was recuperating from the birth, Clementine accepted to herself that she was afraid of Charles. She remembered with horror the day he tried to kick her because she praised the portrait he disliked, but, as always, she tried to excuse him, telling herself that he'd lost his temper because of the oppressive heat and the long tiring sitting he'd endured. He had also not been sober and that always brought out the worst in him.

Perhaps it was her own fault that he'd snapped as he did because she gave him too much wine and she knew that drink made him behave in an unpredictable fashion. She'd seen him burst into uncontrollable furies at servants and members of his entourage when he'd been drinking heavily. He'd once beaten a page to the ground with a stick for looking at him with what he called an insolent eye.

Her father and uncles had all been mild men, under the thumbs of the women of their family, and she'd never seen behaviour like Charles' before, but perhaps princes were different because they were spoiled and indulged from the day they were born.

For her own safety, she determined it was up to her to keep him calm and not antagonize him. While she dearly loved her little daughter, she made up her mind that she would never allow Charlotte to become as headstrong and uncontrollable as her father.

When she was on her feet again, she was so loving and attentive to him that their time together was once more idyllic. Over the weeks of winter he surprised everyone by also being loving and attentive both to Clementine and the baby, who grew fat, pink-cheeked and pretty. The delighted parents passed her to and fro between them like a little doll, and Charles gave her the pet name of Pouponne.

'My Pouponne, my pretty Pouponne, my precious Pouponne,' he cooed, kissing the child's cheeks and marvelling at the beauty of her little hands and feet.

While he crooned and chuckled over his baby, however, he showed no sign of officially accepting her as his legitimate daughter. This worried Clementine who eventually summoned up enough courage to ask him one morning, 'Have you written to tell your father that you have a child, my dear?'

He shook his head. 'There's no need. He'll know. He and my brother know everything that goes on in this household. Their spies tell them.'

'Spies? In this house? Who are they?'

'All of them – especially Goring.'

'But Goring is your secretary and he's very loyal to you. He'd die for you,' she protested because she was sure of Goring's loyalty and in fact often felt that he was jealous of her because of her closeness to the Prince.

Charles sneered, 'You're very naïve. Anyone, even Goring, can be seduced by money. How do I know that my brother has not won you over to his side?' he snapped.

Tears filled her eyes. 'How can you think such a thing of me? I would never betray you,' she said vehemently.

'That's what all traitors say,' he answered.

'I gave up my life and my reputation for you,' she retorted.

'You hadn't much to lose,' he said cruelly.

That night she decided that if her daughter was not going to be officially recognized, she had to at least be christened. When this was suggested Charles ignored what Clementine said and she realized he would do nothing about it, so the decision was up to her. Her religious faith overcame her anxiety not to antagonize the Prince.

'I want our child to be received into the Church. She is almost three weeks old and it's time for her to be baptized,' she told him.

'I don't care whether she is or not. As you know I am not a Roman Catholic any longer. I converted in London,' he replied.

'But you're still a Catholic in your heart. I hear you saying your prayers. I know it. If our daughter is not properly baptized she'll be in danger of going to damnation,' she protested in tears.

'Then christen her if that's what you want but don't go to the local church here in case my enemies get to hear about it,' he said. *Those faceless enemies again!* she thought. He seemed to see them at every turn and used the fear of them to his own advantage.

'Will you come to the christening ceremony and accept our daughter as yours?' she asked him but he shook his head.

'No. I am not a Catholic. Register her as the child of Count and Countess Johnson because that is how people here know us.'

'But Johnson is not your name. Will you not grant her the right of being your legitimate child?'

'You are not my wife. We have never married. How can she be legitimate?'

She flinched but her determination to have Charlotte received into the Catholic church was stronger than her fear of Charles. It was obvious that he loved their child and she was sure that in time he would publicly accept her as his.

'If you don't want the ceremony to take place in our local church I'll ask the priest in the next parish to do it and I'll take her there myself,' she told him.

'To which church?'

'Saint Marie des Fontes.'

'That's not far away. You can take her there and have it done whenever you decide.'

'But won't you at least come with us?'

He became deliberately obtuse and said again, 'No. I'm a Protestant so I cannot enter any Roman Catholic church and Saint Marie des Fontes is Catholic, is it not?'

'But I want my child to belong to the true Church.'

'If you baptize our child as a Catholic it will be against my wishes.'

She saw the look come into his eye that showed he was spoiling for a fight. He wanted her to argue. Though she bowed her head and went quiet she was determined not to give in. She wanted Charlotte to be taken into the protection of her God so next day she carried the well-wrapped child to Saint Marie des Fontes where the priest anointed her and gave her the name of Charlotte Walkinshaw Johnson.

Her father, Charles Edward Stewart, did not attend the ceremony.

Before the week was out, news of the baby's baptism reached Charles' father in Rome and a flood of letters made their way back to Liège.

'Have you accepted this child? Have you married the mother? Are you aware that that woman is spying on you for her sister who lives in the Hanoverian court?' demanded the Old Pretender.

The last accusation festered in Charles' brain because he was already obsessed with the idea that everyone was spying on him and he was only too ready to add Clementine to his list of suspects.

It suited him to have her around however because she jumped to his every command and also he took real pleasure in playing with the child. How pretty the little thing was when it held out its hands to him and chuckled if he pulled funny faces. He lifted it out of its nursemaid's arms and threw it to the ceiling, catching it and holding it tight so that it could not fall or be frightened. The child enjoyed those exploits and the first word she ever uttered was 'Papa'.

As he became more and more besotted with his daughter, however, he lost interest in Clementine. He rarely went to her bed and did not seem to care if she never had another child by him. Many times she rose in the morning to discover that her husband had taken off on one of his mysterious expeditions without telling her where he was going before he left or where he had been when he came back many days later.

He was always complaining about being short of money and complained continually about the expense of keeping up his household. His carping and penny-pinching led to heated arguments between them because Clementine was embarrassed at being unable to pay the bills of local tradespeople.

When the butcher came to protest that he had not been paid for two months, she asked Charles for money and he grabbed her round the throat, almost throttling her. One of the footmen pulled him off her and she was convinced he'd saved her life.

Again she forgave her lover and made excuses for him. Money worries were plaguing his mind, she told herself, and again he had been drinking heavily the day she told him about the overdue butcher's bill. He was never aware of what he was doing when he was drunk. She paid the butcher out of her own dwindling funds.

When Charlotte was almost six months old, Charles burst into Clementine's room one day and shouted, 'Pack your boxes. We're leaving here.'

She sat up in bed bleary-eyed and asked, 'Where are we going?'

He picked a heavy book off the end of the bed and hurled it at her head, missing by inches. 'That's none of your concern. I've had a letter telling me that spies are on my trail. We must leave at once. Get the child ready. Hurry if you know what's good for you.'

Though it was not yet nine o'clock she could see that he had been drinking so she did as she was told.

Their progress from Liège was fast and headlong, going first to Lorraine and then to Paris where Clementine would have liked to stay, for the smart life of the French capital entranced her.

It seemed to suit Charles too because in spite of still complaining about having no money, he went out and began spending lavishly on luxurious new clothes, fans, ribbons, laces – all for himself. He also bought a bejewelled watch and a powerful microscope, though what he intended to do with such an object was a mystery.

The bills were sent to his father in Rome. 'He has plenty of money. The Crown jewels of England are still under his bed. He can sell some of them and pay my bills. I'm his son and it is only right that I live in some style even though he scrapes along like a pauper,' said Charles grandly.

He kept trying to have a public audience with the French king but the wily Louis XV evaded him and sent word that he should quit Paris as soon as possible. This sent Charles into a fury and he was determined to stay on because he was feted in the city by a collection of French Jacobites who filled his mind with thoughts of launching another expedition into Scotland.

Clementine was very much against this idea, because she knew how badly it would be received at home, but Charles' coterie of new friends took against her and whispered that he should get rid of her since she was attempting to control his actions in the Hanoverian interest. Again the story went round that she was spying on him for her sister in London. Charles listened to the whisperers and made it obvious that he was only tolerating his mistress. At every opportunity he would start an argument with her, especially when they were in public.

They were in a café in the Bois de Boulogne one morning when she complained about his recent lavish spending on embroidered waistcoats and lace ruffles while their landlord was complaining about unpaid rent. With a terrible roar, he leaned across the table and threw the contents of his glass of wine in her face. She leaned so far back in her chair that she fell over and he stood up to attack her again but his secretary Goring jumped up too and grabbed him by the arm. 'Remember who you are, my lord. Everyone is staring at you. Sit down and behave like a gentleman,' he said.

Charles looked around and saw a circle of scandalized faces looking in his direction. With bad grace he sat down while Clementine gathered herself together and left the café. Before he returned to their lodgings however he dismissed Goring from his service.

'But I have been with you for years and I have served you faithfully,' Goring protested.

'I have no need of you any longer. Get out of my sight,' was Charles' reply.

'You've lost your supporter. I've sent Goring packing,' he told Clementine when he went back to their lodgings that night.

'But he's the most loyal man that you have about you.'

'He knows too many secrets. He's been in touch with my brother and sends reports to my father. I don't want people like him clinging to me like a leech. You're a leech as well,' he sneered.

She stared at him in horror and protested, 'But I love you. I've always loved you. I left my home and my family for your sake. In spite of what has happened I still love you!' It was true. She did love him. He was the love of her life and she was prepared to forgive him for the way he behaved towards her. She told herself that he had not told her to go so it must mean that he still wanted her to be with him.

Besides, the hard truth was that she had nowhere to go. By sneaking away to join him she had cut herself off from her family. Her money was almost gone and she had her daughter to look after. The baby was the centre of her existence and she knew that if she left Charles, he would never allow her to take the child with her. Where could she go? If she ran away, he would chase her down till he found them because he genuinely doted on his Pouponne, and she returned his affection.

Next day word came from the French court that King Louis would prefer it if Charles Edward Stewart left Paris immediately. It was not a request. It was an order to go and added to it was an inducement. If he went at once, his outstanding bills would be paid for him.

They left that night.

Their next stopping place was Basle just over the Swiss border from France. It was a good situation for Charles because it was easy to travel to other parts of Europe from there and he was more often away from home than he was with his family.

Where he went and what he did, Clementine was never told and he never took her with him.

The cool clear air of Basle, and the hearty Swiss food, made colour return to her pale cheeks, however. Her figure filled out, and baby Charlotte thrived too, prattling more and more every day and bringing joy to the hearts of both her parents who indulged her every whim.

'I'm happy again. I like it here,' Clementine thought one day as she sat in a quiet cloister of the Munster overlooking the river Rhine with her daughter playing at the feet of the carved elephants that were a unique feature of the cathedral. There was a tremendous feeling of peace in the holy place and for the first time in two years she was relaxed and secure. She and Charles had once again assumed new names and now he was passing as plain Mr Thomson, an English gentleman of modest means with a small family, and he played the part to perfection, for once abandoning his old swaggering and posturing. Because he was calmer and more reasonable with her than he had been for a very long time, Clementine told herself that he had changed and that they would once again be able to live happily together.

Though she continued to write pleading letters to her family, it no longer caused her such anguish when nothing came back in return. She had her beloved child and was with the man she still adored in spite of his faults. He seemed to be drinking less and because the biggest cause of trouble between them had been lack of money, the future again seemed hopeful because their financial troubles lessened after Charles' pleas to his father asking for funds were unexpectedly answered.

What Clementine did not know was that, as a condition for providing finance his father ordered his son to get rid of his mistress. Like so many others, the Old Pretender was convinced she was a Hanoverian spy who was leading his son into bad ways for political reasons. If Charles wanted to be financed in a princely way, Clementine *had* to go.

This insistence was a mistake. Charles had always hated being told what to do, especially by his father, and besides it suited him to keep Clementine. She was his acknowledged mistress and agreeable to anything he wanted. He did not love her. He'd never loved any woman because the main object of his adoration was himself, but she filled his bed when he chose to get into it beside her.

In fact he was sexually frigid, like his manipulative great grandmother Mary Queen of Scots. He liked admiration and drew women to him like a honeypot drew flies, but he had no deep need of a woman in his life though he had a mortal dread of being suspected of homosexual tendencies like his effeminate brother.

Complaisant Clementine was an alibi for him and it was easier to keep her than have to go looking for another mistress who

might be like the troublesome women he had around him before
she came from Scotland to join him.

Through members of their household, Clementine knew that
when Charles went off on his trips, he was trying to drum up
support for another landing in Scotland and these efforts became
even more energetic in 1758 when war broke out between
England and France, and it suited the French king to consider
financing a diversionary attack on Scotland.

He invited Charles to come back to Paris to discuss invasion
plans, and provided him with the passport, which had been denied
him before. Once again Charles, Clementine and their baby were
on the move and Basle was left behind them.

She soon discovered that they were going up in the world
once more. No longer did they have to pretend to be the family
of an obscure gentleman. Charles moved into the chateau of
Carlsbourg which belonged to his maternal uncle, the Duke of
Bouillon, and there his mistress and child were to stay while he
travelled to Paris to discuss reviving the Stewart claims.

He was waved off with high hopes by Clementine who thought
as she watched him cantering away across the chateau's park on
a fine charger that she had not seen him looking so handsome
or optimistic for years.

The problem was that his spirits were too high and they stayed
that way. By the time he arrived in Louis' court he was hopelessly drunk. The French king looked at him in obvious distaste,
thinking, 'This man is a fool,' but he knew there were still strong
Jacobite feelings in the north. If Charles could be used to provoke
the English and divert them even if only temporarily from the
war in Canada where most of the fighting was going on, it would
be worthwhile providing him with some ships, men and money.

To Charles' more sober advisers he laid out his plans. 'I'll give
him a fleet of ships and twenty-five thousand men if he starts a
rising in Ireland but the organization will have to be done by you.'

It was a good offer and when Charles' head was more clear,
his advisors laid it before him, but to their bitter disappointment,
he seemed to have completely lost interest in the project.

'I will not go to Ireland. I want to land in Scotland. But I
can't go now because I'm ill,' he announced and took to his bed
where he stayed for a week moaning and groaning.

'What exactly is wrong with him?' his friends and supporters, who were to organize the expedition, asked Charles' faithful and long-suffering valet Faubourg.

The man shuffled his feet and said, 'He cannot sit up.'

'If he can't sit up how does he expect to lead a rebellion? What exactly is the matter? Is he drinking heavily again?'

'Not any worse than usual,' Faubourg said.

'Then what is wrong?' Stafford was insistent.

'He has piles.'

Stafford threw up his hands in despair. 'Piles! The Young Chevalier has piles and can't take up the French king's offer of providing him with an expeditionary force. I'm leaving him now and you can tell him why.'

When Charles returned to Carlsbourg he knew he had let himself down completely and his temper was worse than it had ever been before. He vented most of it on Clementine, who learned to curl up like a beaten animal whenever she heard his voice. He attacked her without mercy, day after day, often beating her senseless while his servants looked on in horror but were unable to stop him. Bruises and scratches marked her body all the time and she had to hide from outsiders or, when badly beaten, avoid emerging from her chamber in daylight.

Because Charles' father James could not get any replies to the many letters he was still sending his son, he despatched a special envoy called Andrew Lumisden to Bouillon with a message and an offer.

When Charles listened to what Lumisden had to say he summoned Clementine and told her, 'Listen to this message from my father.'

She bent her head and sat silent and submissive while he leaned forward gleefully to tell her, 'My father says I must send you away and never see you again. He has offered to maintain you and the child in a secure convent where you will be closely confined and not able to get out and bother me any longer.'

She raised tear-filled eyes and stared at him. This person was so different from the handsome young man she had fallen in love with long ago. He looked older than his years, his face was fat and flushed, his mouth loose, his eyes bloodshot and cruel. It was obvious too that he enjoyed taunting her.

'My father has sent this man here to tell me that you are a Hanoverian spy and I must get rid of you. He thinks I should confine you in a very strict convent and not a comfortable one like the place at Douai. He'll find you a convent where they won't even let you out of the parlour, far less out of the house. If I do as he asks, he'll give me money, so why should I keep you? You're plain and dull and you can't give me a son.'

Lumisden, an arch plotter who loved gossip and intrigue, had believed the scurrilous tales about Clementine but now he saw that she seemed completely broken and did not reply to the insults and threats, only sobbed and cringed whenever Charles made a move towards her. This cringing especially did not go unnoticed by him and he began to feel pity for the weeping woman who he had been told was a cunning spy and manipulator.

It struck him that the situation was different to what his master James believed and he reported on that when he eventually returned to Rome.

But in spite of her pitiful state there was still some inner steel left in Clementine and she began making her own plans.

The only place where she felt safe from Charles was the chapel of the chateau because he ostentatiously avoided entering it and she began spending hours there, kneeling in prayer from which she received much consolation.

First of all, she decided, she must accept that she had made a terrible mistake by falling in love with the Prince and running away from her family to join him.

But I did love him – and he loved me in the beginning. He said such sweet things to me. He said I was the only person in the world who could give him pleasure . . .

The memories that ran through her mind soothed her for a while but were soon dispersed when she forced herself to accept that if she did not escape from him soon, he would probably end up killing her. As it was, he had recently broken one of her ribs and whenever she breathed she had a terrible stabbing pain in her right side. It was not the first time he had broken her bones.

I must get away and I must take Charlotte with me . . .

That was essential. She would never leave without her child. Charles was fond of the little girl too but who could tell how long that fondness would last? He'd been fond of Clementine herself in the beginning and now he was a monster to her. Charlotte must be taken away from him and given a good Christian education.

But I have no money . . . how can I escape without money?

Clementine's inheritance had long gone but she still had a few influential friends left and knew that among the Jacobite visitors who came and went in Charles' circle, there were people who felt sorry for her. Who among them could she trust? She knew only too well that gossip travelled from Charles' establishment to his father and brother as fast as a man could ride. Though he had never told his father about her existence or the birth of their child, he knew every detail.

After a lot of thought she composed a letter to James, the Old Pretender. It was both moving and genuine and when he read it Charles' father realized that the woman he had heard so many bad things about was actually a good and sensible person.

She wrote that she knew he wanted her to leave his son and agreed to do that because she felt that her continued presence in Charles' entourage was working to his disadvantage. If she left it would stop the rumours about her betraying his secrets. She did not say that another reason for her wish to leave was because of Charles' ill treatment of her. In fact she did not say a bad word about him at all but James had heard the stories and knew about Lumisden's observations, so he respected her restraint.

She asked for help in finding a suitable place of refuge where her daughter would be given a Catholic education. This struck a good note with James as well because he was still deeply resentful about Charles' abandonment of the true religion.

This letter was sent off in secret without enlisting the help of anyone, even a servant, and then Clementine waited and prayed. At the same time she wrote another letter to George Keith, the Earl Marischal of Scotland, who was a friend of her father and who had always been kind to her when she was a child.

I need some money to help me escape from a life of tyranny, and I am afraid that if I do not get away soon I will die, she told him.

When Keith read her words he knew she was telling the truth because he had heard rumours as well. He acted at once by sending a message telling her to act with speed and devising a

scheme by which money was passed in secret to her by a Scottish
visitor to the chateau.

With a small bag of coins clinking at her waist she went to
the chapel and knelt in prayer. *Thank you, thank you, oh thank
you,* she said over and over again to the figure of Christ on the
Cross.

She had another reason to give thanks a few days later when
a message came from Rome to tell her that James had been
moved by her letter and if she could get to the French capital,
he had made arrangements for her to be helped by the Archbishop
of Paris.

Showing great resolution and determination, she arranged to
hire a coach to take her to Paris, over a hundred miles away.
Fortunately Charles went off on one of his mysterious visits
abroad and in the middle of the night, she wrapped a cloak round
her precious six-year-old daughter, told her to make no noise for
fear of rousing the servants, and they escaped from Carlsbourg.

On her bedside table she left a letter for Charles in which she
explained why she was leaving him after their eight years together.

> *Because of your constant ill treatment of me my health is suffering
> and I am in daily fear of losing my life. I know I am taking a
> desperate step in removing myself and our child from you but I
> have no alternative and I know that no other woman in the world
> would have suffered what I have undergone.*
>
> *You may rest assured that I will never talk badly of you or
> commit a dirty action against you because in spite of all that has
> happened I still love you. I am leaving you with the greatest regret
> and sincerely wish you health and happiness in the future.*

Then she added a postscript telling him not to wreak vengeance
on any member of the household or any servant for helping her
get away because she had arranged everything by herself.

It was a very dignified and reasonable letter but when he
returned two days later and read it he gave a roar like an enraged
bull and began smashing all the pictures and china in her room.

'I'll catch her and kill her. How dare she take my daughter!
When I find the child I'll have her branded on the forehead
saying she's mine. I'll mark her like a sheep or a cow,' he yelled

and it did not strike him as illogical that he was prepared to brand as his own a child that he would not agree to legitimize officially in spite of Clementine's frequent pleading that he should.

He sent off messengers to Paris because he learned she had hired a coach to go there and he also wrote to the head of the Parisian Police and to the Principal of the Scots College in Paris, ordering them to have every convent searched for his child and her mother. If they were not found, he threatened, he would have every convent in the city burned to the ground. That was a pointless threat and everyone except Charles himself knew it.

When the Archbishop of Paris heard about Charles' ravings, he warned Clementine to leave her lodgings in the Hotel St Louis where she was passing herself off as Madame du Bois and arranged for her to take refuge in a convent at Meaux, about twenty-five miles out of the city.

Frustrated in his efforts to find her, and forbidden to enter Paris by the King, Charles could only storm and fume until he took his usual escape route and drank himself into a daily stupor. For the meantime at least Clementine and her daughter were safe.

Seven

Marion was right about her daughter's fecundity and Flora produced five children – four sons and one daughter – in the seven years that she and Allan spent in the rough and ready conditions of their cramped and basic first home.

With children everywhere and constant demands for food and clean clothes, there was no time for looking back, no time for remembering her adventures, but in spite of working from dawn till darkness, Flora was happy because she was in love with her husband and their children were a constant source of delight to her.

She was leaning over an enormous washing tub with her skirts kirtled up to her knees while she and Chrissie poked at soaking bed sheets with long wooden poles when she heard a horse come galloping into the yard in front of the house door. She stood upright and pushed wet hair out of her eyes with a bare forearm as she peered out of the wash-house door to see Allan come running towards her with a huge smile on his face.

'Florrie, Florrie, here's some good news. My father's giving up his place as Kingsburgh's factor and I'm to take his place,' he cried.

Allan's father was now a widower in his seventies and none too well so they'd known for some time that he would have to stop working soon but it had never been certain that his son could expect to be appointed in his place. That was at the discretion of their clan chief, young Lord James Macdonald who rarely appeared on the estate.

'Are you sure?' she asked, because her husband was apt to be too optimistic sometimes.

'I have it in writing from the young laird,' he said with a huge laugh, taking her hands and sweeping her off into a sort of wild dance. She smiled back, delighted to see how happy he was and, as always, his handsomeness excited her. Constant childbearing and hard work had spread her hips and put thread-like wrinkles on her face but his hair was still jet black and his figure as slim as a swordsman's. She was proud and grateful to be his wife.

When they stopped dancing, she stood panting a little and asked hopefully, 'Does this mean we can move into the big house?'

'Yes, Father suggested that. He wants to stay with us and he's offered to pay for his keep. He's always enjoyed your cooking, but you won't have to do too much of that any more. We'll have plenty of servants so you can start being a lady of leisure and do some entertaining. As factor's wife you'll have the chance to get out your fine tablecloths and polish up your silver. You can give tea parties!' laughed Allan. His recently deceased mother had been well known locally for the lavish splendour of her entertaining.

Flora frowned. Party giving seemed beyond her now and she asked, 'Who is going to come and take tea with me? You know the local ladies don't like me because of what the laird's mother says about me.' Lady Margaret had never stopped castigating Flora for introducing the Young Pretender to her house and for the trouble that followed in his wake.

'You would never have caught our factor's son as your husband if it hadn't been for your Jacobite money,' Lady Margaret openly accused Flora but, because her antagonism did not extend to Allan, for whom she had a soft spot, she never castigated him. As far as she could see he did the right thing by marrying for money; it was only a pity that he had to take 'that gypsy girl' as part of the bargain.

Allan ignored all the slights and whispers. He loved Flora and appreciated her sterling qualities so he defended her stoutly if he heard anyone talking against her. In time the open carping by most people stopped, but hidden resentment remained.

'Forget about her ladyship. She's hardly ever here anyway because she prefers living in Edinburgh. When you're the factor's wife, all the ladies in the district will be coming to visit you. You'll be able to take off that apron and be a lady of style again like you were when you lived in London,' Allan told his wife.

Flora shook her head. She had no wish to go back to her London life. Memories of taking tea and making conversation with Lady Primrose and her friends came rushing back. All they wanted was to hear her tell about the flight across Skye with the Prince dressed up as Betty Burke, her Irish maid. They'd laughed and clapped their hands in delight when she told them about lecturing him because he always forgot to take ladylike steps and went striding out across the heather with his skirts held up at his knees. People they met on their journey raised their eyebrows and wondered what sort of woman she had engaged as a maid.

What she did not tell her appreciative Jacobite audience in London was that he would never take a telling and went striding along because he was drunk from morning till night. One man in their party had to be given the job of carrying his bottles of brandy. Flora was never sure where they came from but she certainly knew where they went.

Neither did she tell them of his petulance and fits of bad temper. He seemed unaware of the sacrifices people were making on his behalf and accepted loyalty as if it was his birthright but she had to admit he never showed any real fear though she herself lived in constant terror of being discovered by a troop of redcoats. And when they parted for the last time, he'd waved a light hand at her as if she had taken a turn on the dance floor with him.

Perhaps all princes feel superior, she thought. *It must be a great help in getting through life.*

Allan saw from her face that something had sobered her and gave her cheek a tender pat as he said, 'Smile again for me, Florrie. You're Kingsburgh's factor's wife now.'

She beamed back at him. 'Congratulations. You deserve the position and you'll do it very well.'

It was pointless, and not something she did very often, to let her mind go back to the days when she was the famous Flora Macdonald, saviour of the Prince. Those days were over and now she had the new task of being a helpful wife to Allan in his post as factor to Sir James Macdonald. His father had held the position for forty years with great success and profit to his master. Till now his father had also taken all the important decisions because Allan tended to be reckless.

She hoped that Allan would become more efficient with the increased responsibility. In spite of her continuing infatuation with him, there was a niggling worry about that at the back of her mind and she decided it would be her task to steady him.

Standing on tiptoe she threw her arms round his neck and kissed him on the lips. 'Well done, well done, husband. You're the new factor now and I'm very proud of you,' she said.

Two weeks later they left their little cottage and in their new home they threw a party to celebrate Allan's elevation in the world. All their neighbours crowded in to drink whisky and empty the bottles of claret that Allan ordered from Edinburgh for the occasion. Fiddlers played and Flora, beaming with pride, moved about among the guests in the Royal Stewart gown that she'd last worn when she was married. The seams had to be let out a little but it still looked very good. She was aware that many of the women were eyeing her critically, but she did not care because she knew that no matter what she did, she would never be able to win them over. Her main concerns were her husband and her children. They were the only people she must worry about.

Coming off the floor after a vigorous reel, she felt a hand on her arm and turned to see her stepfather at her side. He gestured with his forefinger and led her into a little room beside the kitchen.

As always she felt a chill of fear as she followed him because she never quite knew what he was going to say.

'Your fortune is changing, I see. You'll be living in good style now, Florry,' he drawled as he grinned wolfishly at her.

'Allan's done very well,' she said defensively.

'Sir James has a high regard for his father,' said Hugh.

She bristled. Was he implying that Allan had secured his job through nepotism?

'And for Allan. Sir James knows his worth,' she snapped.

'The old man's living with you now, isn't he? He'll be able to keep an eye on what his son's doing. Where is his lordship now?'

'I understand that he's travelling in Italy,' she said.

'Yes, so I hear. Travel is expensive so what he needs is money and it will be your husband's responsibility to see that he gets it. Is there any news about when Sir James is coming back?'

'We don't know. He's travelling with the young Duke of Buccleuch, apparently.'

'Hmm, expensive travel and expensive company. What are they doing exactly – buying up Roman statues?' Hugh grinned.

'I think they're studying because they're travelling with a tutor, a Professor from Edinburgh called Adam Smith.' She was flustered by his cross-questioning and wondered what he was getting at.

'Professors make expensive travelling companions too. As expensive as a stable full of fine horses. The Buccleuchs can afford it but can the Macdonalds of Skye? Your Allan will have to provide a big income for his master. Is he aware of what will be expected of him?'

'Of course he is. He'll do his best for Sir James, you can be sure of that.' Flora was very defensive.

Hugh leaned closer to her and asked in a different tone, 'How much of your dowry money is left, lass?'

She shook her head. 'I don't know. Allan handles all that.'

'You should ask him. He's been dealing in his own right in black cattle recently, hasn't he?'

'Yes.' She knew that Allan bought black cattle from farmers all over the Western Isles and sent them down in droves to Edinburgh's cattle market. His private dealing had been going on for some time.

'If I were you I'd advise him to hold back in the cattle market a bit. He buys too many and pays too much. Some people are taking advantage of his good nature,' said Hugh.

A shiver swept over her for she knew that recently Allan had been sending down a thousand head of cattle at a time but she never heard whether they made good prices or not. She didn't ask because it was not her business, she reckoned. Allan always seemed light-hearted about the business and she trusted him.

Hugh is only trying to worry you. He likes worrying people, she told herself, and decided to concentrate on the good things about her new life. What a delight it was to be mistress of a big house and not a cramped cottage where her children had to sleep three to a bed. Kingsburgh House was roomy and well furnished and she and Allan went to bed every night in the same bed that the Prince had slept in. The sheets he'd used were saved unwashed by her mother-in-law and one was used as her winding sheet when she was buried.

Allan's father lived in a big room on the first floor and for a couple of years he was able to help his son with the administration of the estate, but gradually his memory began to fail and he fretted if he forgot people's names or repeated himself several times in an hour. He grew thinner and more distracted but Flora spent a lot of time with him because she was pregnant again and they used to sit peacefully side by side at his bedroom window companionably staring out at the sea.

He sometimes thought she was his dead wife and one day he told her, 'I'm worried about Allan. He's rash in his dealings and too trusting of the wrong people.' To reassure him she patted his hand and told him not to worry. Allan was doing well, she said.

Then the old man's heart began to give out and he had to fight to draw breath. When Flora was in labour with her sixth child, who turned out to be a boy called John, the old man died of heart failure.

She had loved her father-in-law because he was a kind and gentle man and as she nursed her new baby, she had the strange feeling that his tender soul had entered into the child who came into the world at the same time as he was going out.

A year later John was followed by another baby, a little girl who they christened Fanny. Flora was very tired after the birth and sat half-drowsing in the sun with the baby on her lap on an afternoon when she saw Allan striding through the garden gate and coming towards the house. As always her heart rose at the sight of him, for he was as tall and straight as a pine tree, with his hair still tied back in a long queue. He hadn't aged a day since they were married. She began smiling as he entered the house but the smile froze on her face and disquiet filled her when she saw how worried he looked.

'What's the matter?' she asked in a frightened tone.

'I've just heard the most terrible news,' he told her.

She looked around in a panic wondering where her children were. Were they all safe?

'What about? Is it one of our bairns?' Her voice was breaking so he grabbed her hand in reassurance. 'No, no, it's about Sir James the young laird.' Allan's voice broke as he spoke, for he was obviously distraught.

'What's happened to him?' she asked.

'He's dead. He died in Rome. Word has just come. His mother sent a rider to tell me.'

'But he's only a laddie.' Flora could not believe their laird was dead.

'He was twenty-four but death can come at any time. I thought it might have been another shooting accident like the one he had last year, but the message said he died of a fever. Rome's bad for them apparently.'

'Oh, Allan, that's terrible. He was such a fine young man and a good laird to us. His mother must be in despair.'

'She is. Her other son's the new laird and he will be arriving soon. Her note said he'd be over here to see me as soon as he can.'

'You mean young Donald?' Flora remembered that young man as being very unlike his courteous, unassuming brother.

'Yes, he's twenty-one and he succeeds to the title and the estate.' They both went silent as they thought about this. Donald was a bullying young man who swaggered around a lot and spat out orders to his underlings but, till now, he'd spent most of his time in Edinburgh and only appeared on Skye when he wanted funds. He had not bothered his brother's factor till now.

'I think he's only interested in money,' said Flora slowly.

Allan nodded. 'I agree. He's not really interested in the estate – just in how much he can get off it. He's coming to Kingsburgh tomorrow to talk to me about money matters,' he said slowly and she could tell by his tone of voice that he dreaded this meeting.

'Don't worry about meeting him, Allan,' she said to reassure him, and stood up shifting the drowsing baby on to her hip. He looked down at her because she was much shorter than him but in spite of the difference in their heights, he seemed to quail and he shuffled his feet uncomfortably. Sometimes there was a steeliness about his wife that intimidated him, as it had once intimidated Bonnie Prince Charlie.

'What is wrong? Is there something else you want to tell me?' she asked when she saw his discomfort.

'Oh, Florrie, it's just that I owe the estate some money and with him coming here so soon there just isn't time . . .' His voice trailed off, leaving the sentence unfinished.

'Time for what?' she wanted to know.

'To find enough to pay it all back at once.'

'How much money is involved?' she persisted and because he stayed silent she asked the question again. 'How much, Allan?'

'A lot.'

'*How much?*'

'Five thousand pounds.'

She gave a gasp and sat down on the nursing stool with a thud, which made the baby wake up and start to yell. When she heard it crying, Chrissie ran out from the house and took it from its mother. She could tell by the charged atmosphere between husband and wife that she should not linger.

'Five thousand!' Flora sounded disbelieving and desperate at the same time. Then she glared up at him and asked, 'What did you need all that money for?'

'My black cattle. I sent two thousand eight hundred head of cattle south in the last batch but they were in poor condition when they arrived and made poor prices. When Sir James heard that I was in trouble, he lent me five thousand pounds and now his brother wants it back and I can't pay. Sir James would never have asked for it back all at once till I was ready but Donald is a different matter.'

'My God, you must have bought all the black cattle in the Islands,' Flora said bitterly, remembering One-Eyed Hugh's scornful glee when he talked about Allan's cattle dealing.

'Almost all,' he agreed and she closed her eyes trying to imagine what the cattle cavalcade looked like as it wended its way down through the Scottish countryside to Edinburgh's meat market.

'Don't you worry. I'll pay it back,' Allan hastened to reassure her.

'Exactly how?' she asked. The bulk of her dowry money was gone by now, she was sure.

'When the new laird comes here I'll tell him the truth about poor sales and ask for time to repay my debt,' he said hopefully.

'I agree Sir James would have given you time but I doubt if his brother will be as tolerant. He's a money grabber and the estate here doesn't mean so much to him. He doesn't like Skye and never has done. After he went to school in Edinburgh he's hardly been back.'

'We went to the same school,' said Allan, as if that was going to forge a bond between them, but Flora shook her head.

'That won't influence him when he finds that you owe him five thousand pounds.' She didn't dare even say the words but she was thinking that Allan might be sent packing. He might even go to prison! It was a factor's responsibility to raise as big an income as possible for the estate he managed, and it was certainly forbidden to help himself to any of the funds. 'Why didn't you tell me what you were doing?' she asked mournfully.

'It didn't all go at once. I meant to repay Sir James but he didn't press me so I spent most of it buying bigger lots of cattle to try to make up my losses. I'll pay it back, Flora. I never intended to keep it.'

'I believe you didn't, but will Sir James' brother? Can't we pay back some of it from my dowry money?'

'There isn't much of that left either.' So Hugh had been right. When she realized that Flora felt even worse.

Allan was watching her as if he expected her to come up with some solution but all she could say was, 'You've been a fool, Allan.'

'I know. What can I do?' he asked her like a child.

'All you can do is throw yourself on his mercy and undertake to pay back every penny. When is he expected here?'

'By midday tomorrow. We must put on a good spread for him.'

She grimaced. 'Any spread we can put on today will have to be washed down by ale. We can't give him whisky or claret in case he thinks we're living above our income.'

'Your home-brewed ale is very good,' said Allan and for once his compliment did not make her smile.

The midday interview next day was as uncomfortable as Allan feared. Flora stayed in the kitchen with the servants while her husband spoke with his employer in the upstairs drawing room. From time to time she heard a raised voice and it was always the new laird's.

'I've come to see you because of the rumours that you have had no success with your cattle dealing. I hope you've not been risking my money,' the young man said as a start to their interview.

'Oh no, any losses have been my own. The estate is not involved,' Allan told him.

'That's just as well but there's something else. In my brother's papers I found this.' He laid a sheet of paper on the table between them and without examining it Allan knew what it was – a receipt signed by him for the loan he got from Sir James.

'It means that you owe my estate a lot of money,' said the laird coldly.

'And I will pay you back. Your brother said he was prepared to wait until my cattle showed a profit.'

'That might be never. My friends tell me you have been losing money for at least three years. My brother was not businesslike in his dealings with you but I'm not prepared to wait as long as that for my money. I need it now.'

'Will you let me pay it bit by bit?' Allan hated to have to plead.

Sir Donald eyed the man standing in front of him. He'd known Allan and his father all his life and also knew the respect in which the old man was held by his father and brother. The son was a different case though. He seemed foolishly optimistic and lacking in business acumen.

'Give me one reason why I should not dismiss you,' he said sternly. Though he was young he was secure in his confidence because of his social position.

'I am loyal to you and your family. My father was loyal to you all his life. If you give me the chance to repay your brother's loan, I will not fail you, but if you turn me away from Kingsburgh I'll never be able to repay the loan,' said Allan miserably. The bit about affording to repay the loan was what swayed his employer.

'I'll give you another chance but you must sharpen up and start paying me back immediately. If you don't you and your family are out of here,' said the young laird, turning away and pulling his bonnet on to his head.

'Thank you, sir. I hope you will stay and take food with us. My wife has been cooking for you,' said Allan.

'Tell your wife I haven't time to waste eating here. All I want is a start of your repayments,' was the discourteous reply.

Allan had anticipated that and had searched out some money in advance. He opened a drawer in the table and pulled out a jingling purse. 'There's a hundred guineas in this. It's a start,' he said, passing the purse over.

Sir Donald pocketed it with the comment, 'Only four thousand nine hundred to go.'

When she heard the laird and his cavalcade of companions clattering away from the courtyard, Flora stopped basting a huge shoulder of mutton that was swinging over the kitchen fire and wiped her brow before she ran upstairs to Allan to ask if they had been granted a reprieve. She did not want to leave Kingsburgh and feared that if they were forced to go, Allan would take her and the family to America where many other Highland families had gone recently. He'd been showing great interest in accounts of life over the ocean that came back to Skye from time to time. 'That's the place for people who are prepared to work,' he told Flora more than once.

He was sitting on a chair beside the big table when she entered the room and he looked totally downcast. 'What did he say?' she asked in trepidation.

'He wants me to pay it all back as soon as possible. I gave him all the money I could scrape together – one hundred guineas,' was the miserable reply.

The money had been put aside to pay Charles' school fees in Edinburgh.

'Charles can stay at home for another year, but what about you? Did he dismiss you as his factor?' said Flora.

'No. He's giving me another chance. Providing that I can go on paying him back I can stay. Sir James would never have done this to me.'

'But Sir James is dead, unfortunately. What are you going to do about raising the rest of the money?' She was distraught but tried to hide her fear.

'I don't know. We'll have to economize. We can do it!' As always Allan was looking on the bright side.

'We're not extravagant but we can go back to eating what's cheap or costs us nothing. The children won't suffer on a diet of oatmeal and herrings and I can let some of the household servants go. Chrissie and I can manage on our own,' said Flora in a determined voice. She was not afraid of hard work.

'I'll be more careful with my cattle buying and take care not to pay too much for them,' Allan told her and she groaned.

'Must you go on with the dealing? It's not been good recently, has it?'

'If I don't we'll never find any extra money. I told Sir Donald to keep my salary as part of my loan repayment.'

'What does that leave us to live on?' asked Flora in a frightened voice.

'Nothing. It leaves us nothing except anything I make by cattle dealing, but don't worry, I'll take care and we'll get through.'

That afternoon Flora took herself off to speak to her mother and stepfather whose house was nearby. She hated having to do it but she intended to ask Hugh for a loan. Annoyingly, he seemed to know what was on her mind before she even uttered the words.

'I heard the new laird was at your house this morning and that he didn't stay long, not long enough to dine,' he said with a grin.

'He came on business, not to eat with us.'

'And was the business concluded satisfactorily?'

'In a way, yes.' She tried to sound confident.

'So Allan is still the factor?'

'Yes.'

'How much does he owe the estate?' asked Hugh.

She had no intention of telling him though she guessed he knew already anyway. 'I don't know,' she lied.

'I can lend you enough money to live on while he's getting his finances sorted out but I'm not paying out any big sums. Your Charles is a clever boy, isn't he, and old enough to find a position in the outside world. We must find him a place. And you should start looking round for a rich husband for your girl Anne, too. She's turning into a beauty so it shouldn't be hard.' Hugh as usual was making plans for other people.

Flora was horrified. 'But she's only fourteen. She can't get married yet.'

'Time passes. She'll be marriageable soon. I'll put out some feelers,' he said for he enjoyed doing things like that and she remembered that it was he who organized her wedding to Allan. In spite of their money problems she would not want to be married to anyone else, so perhaps he'd find a good match for Anne too.

As Flora walked home she thought hard about other ways of

solving their problem and when she went into the kitchen she saw her husband sitting on a bench by the fire with his head despondently in his hands. He looked so hopeless that she was filled with determination and energy, ready to take all the difficult decisions as she had done when she was ferrying Charles away from the redcoats.

'I've decided what to do. We need another loan. From a banker this time,' she told him.

'We don't know any bankers,' he said, looking up.

'I do. When I was in Edinburgh I used to go to visit the family of Mr Murdo Mackenzie who was a friend of my father. He was very kind to me and he's a prosperous lawyer and a banker in the city. I'll write to him and ask him to see you and give you advice about raising a loan to pay off Sir James.'

Mr Mackenzie was a kind man who admired Flora and he wrote back by return offering to advise Allan and telling him to take all his business papers and account books with him when he went to Edinburgh. Allan brightened at the prospect of going to the capital because he loved travelling and often chafed at having to stay at home concentrating on mundane matters. His time at the Royal High School had been very pleasant and he made many friends in the city because he was a gregarious, popular man.

He set off looking magnificent with his plaid draped over his shoulder and was away for a week while Flora spent her time writing letters to other people who she thought might be able to help. One of them was her old friend Lady Primrose.

When Allan returned Flora could tell at a glance that he was not bringing good news. He pulled off his plaid and threw it over a chair by the kitchen fireside, holding his hands up to the flames for warmth because it was bitterly cold outside and frost was silvering the stones of the garden wall.

'How was the journey?' she asked.

'Very hard. I met many people in Edinburgh who send you their regards. You haven't been forgotten down there, my dear.'

She smiled as she said, 'And how was Mr Mackenzie?'

'I didn't see him, I'm afraid.'

She turned round from the cooking fire and stared at him in disbelief. 'You went all that way and didn't see him?'

'I couldn't face him. He's such a great man of business; I was ashamed to let him see what a mess I've made of my affairs.'

She was angry now. 'So you did not keep your appointment with him. That was a terrible discourtesy.' If Allan had been one of her sons she would have boxed his ears. He only shrugged and strode away so she did not get the chance.

When she winkled the details out of him, it turned out that he had met up with a group of jolly old schoolfellows and spent the time in ale houses, totally forgetting his appointment with Mr Mackenzie who wrote to Flora deploring her husband's failure to turn up. She replied with such a heartfelt apology that she succeeded in softening him up enough to offer to intercede with Sir Donald and ask him to agree to a decrease in their rent for Kingsburgh as well as a deferment on the interest which he originally demanded on the capital his brother lent to Allan.

The laird was intransigent, however, and even insisted that Allan's rent would have to be increased and the interest paid in full. A despairing Mr Mackenzie wrote to Flora to say that Allan would be well advised to agree to those terms because Sir Donald was not in the mood to be forgiving and might become even more difficult if provoked. There was no way out. They would have to go on labouring under their burden of debt.

Allan and Flora were both in the depths of despair when a letter arrived from Lady Primrose which showed that her old affection and support for Flora was as strong as ever.

'My dear,' she wrote, 'I have been thinking about your troubles and realize how expensive for you it must be to keep your troop of children at home. It is time that your eldest son should be found a good position in life where he can establish himself as a gentleman. I know from what you have said about him that he is a good and clever boy and he is also named after our dear Prince, which is also good.

'Through contacts I have found him a position as a clerk in the East India Company at Madras. This is a great opportunity for him because boys who go out there penniless can return as nabobs with immense riches. I will pay for his passage and equip him for the journey in the hope that going to India will give him the chance of making good in life and be able in future to help his family at home.'

Flora wept when she read this letter, partly out of gratitude to her old friend, and partly from dread of parting with her eldest son. He was only sixteen years old after all, and still a boy with his voice only half broken. How could he cope with life in Madras? It was true that fortunes were made there but the men who lived to do so were lucky because the diseases of the east were mainly cruel fevers that snatched a sufferer away within twenty-four hours. Charles was strong and sturdy like his father but how would he withstand tropical fevers?

She ran to show Lady Primrose's letter to Allan, who was delighted. 'It shows the high regard she still has for you and it's a great chance for Charles,' he said.

'But what if he's homesick?' Flora asked in anguish.

'Oh he's young, he'll get over it,' was Allan's reply. It was obvious that he did not think for a moment that Charles would turn the offer down.

They went together to break the news to their son who was in the stables grooming their best horse. He had his curly head bent over the horse's foreleg when they stood at the box door watching him. He was still thin and boyish. What sort of man would he make?

Allan broke the news by asking, 'How would you like to go to India, lad?'

Charles looked over with a grin on his face. 'I'd like it fine but there's no chance, is there?'

'Think again. Lady Primrose has arranged a place for you with the East India Company in Madras. Do you want to take up her offer?'

Charles realized his father was serious and stood up slowly with his face solemn. 'I don't think I want to leave home yet. I was very sad when you said you were going to send me to school in Edinburgh and I don't mind that you can't afford to send me now.'

Allan gestured to Flora to go away and walked into the box to stand beside his son and lay an arm over the boy's shoulders. She waited out in the yard till they came out together, both looking very solemn.

'I've decided that I'll go to Madras. It's too good an opportunity to miss,' Charles said to his anxious mother. She looked at her husband who nodded to encourage her, 'He'll do well,' he said.

'Do you really want to go to India? Don't say yes if you have any doubts,' she said to her son.

'I want to go,' he said firmly and she guessed that Allan had told him that if he accepted the position being offered to him, he would greatly relieve the family money worries and put them all in the way of being better off in time.

Charles knew very well that his father was impractical and given to making wrong decisions where money was concerned and he'd heard the local jokes about the black cattle fiasco so he was shouldering his share of the family responsibilities and his childhood was over.

'I really want to go,' he told his mother though he knew that all the time he was away he'd miss his home with a terrible longing.

She held out her hands and grasped his. 'Oh, my dearest son, how I am going to miss you! Will I write to Lady Primrose now and tell her that you accept her offer?'

'Yes, tell her and thank her. I'll do my best not to let her or any of you down when I go away,' he said bravely though he knew that in the steamy heat of Madras he would wake up on many mornings longing for the frosty feel of winter and the drifting sleet and mists of Skye.

Only a month later came the first separation. The whole family went to Edinburgh with Charles and spent the last of their money to purchase a trunk full of necessities for his life in Madras. They bought clothes, hats, books and patent medicines before going down to Leith, the port outside the capital, where the big *East Indiaman* was moored. It looked immense with its masts towering up to the sky and sailors climbing up and down them like an army of ants.

Charles was to share a small cabin for the six-month voyage with three other Company hopefuls and Flora was afraid that there was so little space the boys might suffocate during the night for want of air. 'Always keep the door open when you go to sleep,' she said anxiously and then went to find the captain and ask him to keep a special eye on her dear son who seemed to be so much smaller and punier than his cabin mates.

The captain was accustomed to requests from anxious mothers and made reassuring noises. 'The trip out east always hardens up the lads,' he told her.

She held a letter out towards him and said, 'When you get to South Africa will you be so good as to post this to me so that I know he's at least got there safely?' she pleaded.

He looked at the address on the cover. 'Flora Macdonald, Kingsburgh, Isle of Skye,' he read, then he looked hard at her and asked, 'You're not the Flora Macdonald who saved the Young Chevalier, are you?'

It was a long time since she'd thought of herself in that role. Though she knew that not everyone she met thought she had done the right thing, she decided to tell the truth, nodded and said, 'Yes I am.'

'Why did you help him?' asked the captain.

Her eyes clouded and she thought for a moment. *Why did I do it? How would my life have worked out if I'd refused?* she wondered and remembered seeing the Young Pretender standing tall under the low roof of the bothy. He'd looked filthy and exhausted in the light of the dying fire. 'He wakened my pity. The redcoats were after him and I could not refuse to help a poor soul in distress,' she said.

The bluff captain suddenly grinned and clasped her hand. 'I'm honoured to meet you, Mistress Flora. I'm a Macpherson myself and I've been a firm Jacobite all my life so I've read all the accounts of what you did. You're a brave woman.'

'I'm not so brave now. I'm worried about my boy going off into the world,' she said in a quavering voice.

'Don't you worry about him. I'll keep an eye on the lad for you and yes, I'll post your letter to give you peace of mind.' Then with a courtly gesture he kissed her hand.

She stood with Allan and the rest of her children on the quay while the ropes were cast off and the sails of the ship filled with wind and carried it off into the Firth of Forth. The tears that filled her eyes blinded her and stopped her watching it till it disappeared behind the Bass Rock.

The sight of the tall ship bearing his son away to foreign parts had a strange effect on Allan. It seemed to waken a sort of wander-lust in him and he started talking seriously about going to America.

Because Flora did not want to leave her homeland, she ignored her husband's attempts to lure her into discussion about emigration but she could not ignore the fact of their increasing poverty. Though Allan managed to pay back some of Sir Donald's money, the fact that he also had to pay interest meant that the main sum owing never seemed to get much less. With concern she watched him poring over his account books till late at night. One evening he threw down his pen and sat back in his chair with a groan. 'It's no good, Florrie. We're never going to get out from under this debt. It will be best for everybody if we pack up and go to Carolina.'

That was it. Out in the open. She could not ignore it now. 'Can we afford to go?' she asked.

'If we go soon. We'll have to sell up all our goods and chattels and the stock we have on the farm. That should raise enough money for our fares and set us up over there.'

'I don't really want to go, Allan.'

'But it's our only chance. Sir Donald is against me now and even if I pay off the debt there's no guarantee that he won't send me away me sooner or later. It's best for us to go before that happens,' Allan told her.

Flora sighed and stared into the heart of the fire. 'What will Carolina be like?' she asked.

'I've spoken to people who've been there and they say it's good farming country, with lush fields and tall stands of trees. People there have a comfortable life because the climate's not much different to ours, but with warmer summers and colder winters. There's a lot of Scottish families settled there already so we'd be among our own kind.'

'Do you really want to go?' she asked but she already knew the answer. He very much wanted to go.

'I'll go to Portree and find out how much our passages will cost and then we'll talk about it again. Don't say anything to your mother and One-Eyed Hugh because they'll spread the news and people will think they can pick up our stuff for next to nothing,' he told her.

In spite of his precautions however word soon got round that Allan Macdonald had been in Portree enquiring about the cost of fares to Carolina and gossip raged. He and Flora did their sums and their gloom deepened when they realized that it would be prohibitively expensive to transport themselves and their remaining children across the Atlantic.

Hugh had a partial answer to that. He turned up in their house one morning with a proposition.

'I hear you're thinking about taking to the high seas,' he said to Flora.

'Who told you that?'

'Big Allan Macdonald is easy to spot. When he's on the quay at Portree quizzing ships' captains, the word soon gets round. Have you enough money for all your fares? I doubt it.'

Flora pressed her lips together. If anything was likely to put her on Allan's side and make her eager to go, it was Hugh's interference.

'If we go it won't be for about a year,' she said. She and Allan had decided they needed to make some more money from his cattle dealing before they left.

'You two and all those children. That'll cost a small fortune in fares. I told you I'd ask around for a husband for Anne. What would you say if I told you that a friend of mine wants to marry her? That'll save you some passage money and you'd only have to pay out for a small wedding. He's not asking for any dowry.'

'But Anne's still so young. Who's offering for her?' she wanted to know.

'Macleod of Glendale. His wife died a couple of years ago and your girl's caught his eye. He's well set up and she'd live the life of a lady.' Hugh obviously thought he'd pulled off a coup.

'Macleod! But he must be fifty years old.' Flora was astonished at this proposed marriage, for she and Allan were both only fifty-three.

'He's forty-nine. And sixteen's not too young to be married. Your mother married your father when she was sixteen, and just over twenty when he died, so getting a young husband is not a guarantee that he's going to live long enough to keep you. It's better to marry an older man with money behind him and Macleod's got good family connections as well.'

'I know. He's a bastard of the chief of the clan Macleod, isn't he?'

'Yes and his father acknowledged him and gave him a tack at

Vaternash that brings in a good income. Not only that but his half-brother's just died in India and left him five hundred pounds. He's had an interesting life because he was in the army and served in India and Quebec. It would be hard to find a better catch and if you don't snatch him up for Anne, some other woman will get him.' Hugh was always very matter of fact about marriage and Flora knew that he and her mother would have discussed this matter between them. Marion had done well for herself when she married him only months after being left a poor widow.

'I'll have to ask Anne how she feels about this,' said Flora.

'Take care you point out all the advantages to her,' her step-father replied.

When he was told about the marriage proposal, Allan sided with Hugh and said, 'Anne's maturing fast and it's certain she'll be looking for a man soon. When she marries it might as well be to someone like Glendale who has a lot of wool on his back.' Flora thought that very mercenary but realized that she was the only member of the family who wanted her daughter to be starry-eyed about the man she married.

That night she and Allan kept their daughter behind after the family supper and told her that Macleod of Glendale had made an offer to marry her.

There was a strong physical similarity between Anne and her grandmother Marion and they resembled each other in character as well. Anne was ripe and eager for marriage and wanted to better herself.

Her face lit up when she heard who had offered for her. 'I've seen him. He's a fine-looking man,' she said.

'But he's more than thirty years older than you,' Flora pointed out.

That objection did not carry much weight with her daughter who said, 'And I've heard he's rich.'

'He has a bit of money behind him,' Flora agreed and wondered how much their own straitened way of life had affected their children. Had it made Anne mercenary – or only sensible?

'What do we say to Hugh and Marion about this proposal? Do you want to wait a bit and think about it?' Flora asked but Anne shared her step-grandfather's fear of letting this prize slip through her fingers.

'No, tell him I agree. I'm sorry that I won't be able to go to America with you but by getting married I'll save you the passage money, won't I?' Anne was nothing if not practical.

Allan was determined that his eldest daughter should marry properly and dipped into his emigration money to send her off in style, importing more claret and malt whisky that would be drunk down during the three-day celebration during which a trio of fiddlers and a troop of pipers provided the music.

As handsome as ever, he gave his daughter away and the bride's mother hid her work-worn hands in the folds of the silken skirts of her Royal Stewart gown.

Anne looked magnificent, willowy and dark-haired in a silken gown. The groom wore his years well and stood beside his new wife with a satisfied smile on his face and a Macleod plaid flung over his shoulder as a tribute to his mother-in-law who he thought must be a Jacobite – after all she'd risked her life to save the Young Pretender, hadn't she?

Much to her relief Flora liked him and felt he would be kind to Anne, because it was going to be a bitter wrench when she set sail for America and left her girl behind.

Eight

'When is papa coming back? I want to see my papa.' Charlotte was used to her father disappearing for weeks at a time but when he returned it was as if he brought a rush of excitement through the door with him and he always lavished her with gifts and kisses. She worshipped him and though she loved her mother too, part of her thought that Clementine was deliberately keeping her and her father apart and she hid a deep resentment about that.

With the help of the Archbishop of Paris, Clementine and her child had been granted secure refuge at last at the convent of Notre Dame at Meaux en Brie, almost thirty miles north-west of Paris in a rural part of the country well away from anywhere that Charles may go looking for his runaway family.

She had not joined the order but lived the life of a well-to-do lady in fairly comfortable, but not rich, circumstances. Because she had powerful protectors and because the prioress and several of the nuns admired the aristocracy, even illegitimate members of it, they made much of Charlotte as the daughter of the Jacobite heir, and deferred to her. They told the little girl romantic stories about her father trying to regain his father's kingdom in some country far away. This made her unduly proud and conscious of her background and breeding and all the more anxious to make her mark in society one day.

Every time she asked about her father, her mother seemed to stiffen, which told the eight-year-old child that she was being fobbed off.

'He will be returning soon. He's travelling on serious business. He has many big concerns . . .' The explanations were always vague but accompanied by loving hugs and kisses because Clementine was a doting mother and she wanted to make up for the missing Charles. One thing she would not do however was to call her daughter by the pet name he had invented for her. Now she was Charlotte and no longer Pouponne.

It was Pouponne who wept for her father when she was alone, and she made a firm resolve that one day, somehow, she would meet him again to throw her arms round his neck and kiss him like she used to do. He became a heroic, almost mythical figure in her mind.

Her mother had no desire to go into society and was obsessively anxious to keep out of the limelight and live a quiet life. She did not tell her daughter that she was hiding from Charles' vengeance.

She still wrote to her sisters and her mother without receiving any replies until at last a letter came from one of the sisters telling her to stop writing because as far as her mother was concerned, she was dead and so she must never to try to contact her again. She had made a dreadful mistake and would have to pay for it forever.

Poor Clementine wept over the letter and knew that the only person she had left to love and cherish and be cherished by in return was her daughter. It now became her motive in life to do her best for Charlotte who was proving to be a clever child and an able pupil. Her tutors enthused over her work and that delighted her mother who did not hide or underestimate the facts of Charlotte's background. She was told that she had a grandfather in Rome, who was always referred to by her mother as 'the old gentleman over the hills' and who was rightly a King.

On Charlotte's behalf, for she was anxious that the child should not be overlooked or ignored, Clementine felt it essential to keep in communication with the Old Pretender, and she sent him another carefully worded letter asking for his protection and explaining that she left Charles for two reasons – one being that she wished to put an end to the malicious gossip that said she was a Hanoverian spy and that her presence in the Prince's household was only doing him harm; and secondly – and most importantly, she stressed – because she wanted her daughter to have a decent Christian education which Charles could not provide because of the wandering life that he was leading.

When this letter arrived at the Palazzo Muti in Rome, where

James lived in squalid and parsimonious conditions, he sent a message to his son Henry, Cardinal Duke of York, to come and discuss it with him.

'Read that,' he said, thrusting the letter over the table when Henry appeared.

The cardinal took his time, savouring every word, and then he said, 'This is a surprise. Perhaps she is not as bad as we have been told. In fact she sounds like a sensible and honest woman.'

'But she must be a fool before she ever took up with that idiot son of mine,' was his father's reply. James alternated between berating Charles and grieving that he never saw or heard from him except through third parties. They had not met since 1745 when Charles left to launch his ill-fated attempt at the rebellion in Scotland, a venture of which his father deeply disapproved and indeed forbade. He should have known that to forbid Charles to do anything was a direct invitation for him to start.

'Her letter is well written and very literate. She sounds resolute too. I don't think there's any risk of her going back to him. I've heard stories about how he ill treated her and yet she does not try to justify herself for leaving him on those grounds. That's to her credit. She has dignity,' said Henry while re-reading the letter. Like his father he had believed the tales about Clementine's Hanoverian connections, but now he found himself warming towards the woman and even sympathizing with her. After all she had put up with his brother for eight years.

'I wanted them to part. I thought that he had to be free of her before he could make a respectable marriage with some woman from a family of high status. I did nothing to try to persuade her to go, but at least I arranged for the Archbishop of Paris to give her shelter,' protested James after one of the fits of coughing which regularly interrupted his conversations these days.

Henry told him, 'It's just as well that you did and I hear Lord Keith, who was a friend of her father, also helped. Without him and the Archbishop, it's possible my brother could well have murdered her and that would be an even greater scandal. They say he came close to it several times.'

'Her letter says the child is clever and she flourishes with good teaching but needs more. That takes money and they are probably living in a poor way because she does not come from a rich background,' said James slowly. He hated parting with money but his conscience had been awakened.

Henry was more generous and realistic. 'Then you must make her an allowance, Father. For the child's sake.'

'How much do you think? They are living in a convent, which is not expensive, is it?'

'But they have to pay for their keep and as your granddaughter the child should live up to a certain standard for the sake of our family name. She is Charles' daughter after all. I think her mother needs at least six thousand livres a year,' Henry told him.

'That's more than I pay Lumisden!' protested his father.

'Lumisden would work for you as your secretary for nothing because he is so loyal. It's six thousand, I think,' said Henry firmly.

And so six thousand it was, which kept Clementine and her daughter in reasonable comfort till the girl was fourteen, by which time she had acquired all the talents required of a well-born lady and was cultured and very articulate. The letters she wrote to her grandfather and uncle in Rome so impressed Henry that even after his father died, he kept on paying Clementine's allowance out of his own funds.

With the aid of influential friends in the church Henry also decided that Clementine deserved an elevation in status and she was granted the title of Countess of Alberstrof, which increased her social position, but did not put any more money in her pocket. It did however mean that when Charlotte was old enough she might be able to move into society and perhaps make a decent marriage.

Once or twice over the years Clementine sent a forgiving letter to Charles, admonishing him to look after his health and assuring him that she still loved him. This was true. He was the love of her life and never a day went by without her thinking of him and wondering what he was doing.

Any news that reached the convent about him usually stressed his continued heavy drinking and pointless wanderings to and fro across Europe trying to raise support for another attempt at winning back the throne. She did not worry much about that for she knew him well enough to be aware that if any serious help for rebellion was ever forthcoming, he'd find some way of backing out of the enterprise.

In fact Charles was becoming a figure of mockery and his old hero status had long ago been forgotten by everyone except his mistress and his daughter, the most faithful Jacobites and the romantically minded nuns at Meaux.

Charlotte was his most faithful admirer, and still anxious to make contact with her father. Over the years she wrote him several letters, starting off with childish missives signed by Pouponne but later going on to more elegantly written ones stressing how carefully she was looked after by her mother and saying that she had made good progress in Latin.

One touching letter written when she was fifteen had a post-script added by Clementine which said, 'Our daughter is an adorable child who is very dear to me because she is yours. It is my ambition that she should do you honour and I would die a thousand deaths lest a word slip from my mouth that would do you the slightest injury.'

That was a promise that she stuck to throughout her long life.

Charles never answered any of the heartfelt letters from his mistress or his child.

Nine

Years of melancholy and raging hypochondria made it difficult for even his devoted youngest son Henry to appreciate that James, the Old Pretender, was really dying, but when the doctors confirmed the patient's worst suspicions, he sent off a barrage of letters to Charles pleading with him to come to Rome and say farewell.

'Let me hold your hand again. Let us be reconciled. I long to see you once more before I die,' James wrote pathetically, forgetting the years of animosity and frustrated love. The indifference of his oldest son pained his heart for in spite of constant criticisms of Charles, he was a loving father.

Henry added his pleas to his father's, and stressed that James was really dying and that his dearest wish was to say goodbye to his favourite son. Charles ignored even these heartfelt requests. When he received them, his immediate response was to get drunk.

After months of suffering, on a cold January day in 1766, James Stewart, who claimed to be James III, King of England, Scotland, Ireland and Wales, died in his son Henry's arms. The Cardinal looked down with genuine sorrow at the emaciated dead face and raged in his heart against his brother.

It would not be long, he bitterly guessed, before Charles turned up to claim his father's treasures, because as eldest son he inherited all James' worldly goods, which were considerable in spite of the father's persistent but mistaken belief that he was poor.

'Do you think he will have the grace to arrive in time for the funeral?' Henry's lover Angelo Cesarini, a dean of Frascati, asked.

Henry shook his head. 'I doubt it, but he won't be long after because he'll want to find out how much has been left to him.'

And what he said proved to be true. The old man was buried in the Vatican vaults amid a huge crowd of mourners and Pope

Clement XIII himself conducted the ceremony. Henry walked in front of a vast procession, proud that his father was being paid such a signal honour, and right till the last minute kept on hoping that his brother would make an appearance, but he was to be disappointed. A statue by Canova was later commissioned to mark James III's last resting place.

It soon emerged that miserly old James was worth a great deal of money, even more than Henry suspected. 'This is a great surprise because both he and my mother starved themselves to death,' he said sadly and it was true that James ate the poorest food and drank no wine, while his wife Clemetina Sobieski had starved herself for religious reasons and died of scurvy and malnutrition at the age of only thirty-three.

What offended Henry's pride was that his father had such a huge fortune yet he unashamedly kept on seeking handouts from rich Jacobites who came to pay court to him over the years.

There was one problem which Henry was anxious to solve before his brother turned up. Where were the Crown jewels? He believed that somewhere in the palazzo his father had secreted a selection of priceless items from the English and Scottish Crown jewels that King James II, the Old Pretender's father, smuggled out of England when he was deposed and fled by boat along the Thames in 1688.

In a fit of pique he threw the Great Seal of the Kingdom into the water but kept a selection of other valuable jewel-encrusted items. It was certain that his son, the father of Charles and Henry, had them hidden away.

Henry told Cesarini, 'We must do a search and if we do turn them up, I'll remove them and leave them to you in my will so you can take care of their proper distribution. They have to be kept out of my brother's hands or he'll sell them and squander the money.'

Henry had a strong sense of history and tradition and wanted the precious items to be restored to their proper place but he knew he could not do that while Charles was still alive for he would certainly not want to hand over such valuable treasures.

Not having any claim to a share of his father's fortune did not worry Henry, who was immensely rich anyway as his cardinalate of Frascati was one of the most lucrative in Italy.

'We have to find those jewels before my brother gets his hands on them,' Henry told Cesarini, who nodded in agreement.

'Indeed we must, or they'll be broken up and sold for the stones. Your brother is an endless drain for money,' Cesarini said.

For the whole of one day they searched the dirty and decrepit palace, turning up items in some very unexpected locations, including the golden crown of Mary of Modena, James II's wife, which had been hidden in an ancient commode in an attic. They also found the bejewelled decoration that King Charles I wore round his neck when he went to be executed, as well as the great cross of St Andrew and many enormous jewels – rubies, diamonds and sapphires. They came from the Polish Sobieski collection and Henry decided to leave them for his brother.

With the help of the late James' secretary Lumisden, who loathed Charles, the priceless royal items were whisked away in secret to Frascati only just in time because two days later Henry received a letter signed Charles III – announcing his arrival at the Palazzo Muti and ordering Henry to attend on him there because he had many commissions he wanted carried out.

Though Henry deplored his brother's neglect of their father, it was not his way to go on the offensive, but to behave diplomatically and carefully hide his true feelings. When he arrived at the Palazzo Muti, he was met at the door by an agitated looking Lumisden who said, 'He's here. He's in very high feather.'

Henry frowned. 'Do you mean he's drunk?'

'No, not yet. It's too early. He's ordering everyone around and complaining about the state the place is in. He's commissioned an army of cabinetmakers, upholsterers and decorators already. God knows how much it's going to cost.' Lumisden had been infected with his late employer's parsimony.

Henry laughed as he looked at the paint-flaked walls and threadbare hangings. 'It is a horrible mess now so perhaps he has a point. He can afford it, after all,' he said.

'I don't think you appreciate the scale of his ambitions,' said Lumisden sourly.

'Perhaps I don't. But I want you to stay here as long as you can to try to keep a curb on him,' Henry told the secretary, who groaned.

'I don't know how long I'll be able to stand it. He's already sent half of your father's old retainers packing, and he's boasting about you arranging a meeting for him with the Pope,' was Lumisden's glum reply.

Henry frowned. 'I can't arrange for him to meet the Pope. Any invitation has to come from the pontiff himself, you and I know that.'

'But does your brother? I don't think any Pope is going to invite a man who poses as a Protestant but crosses himself several times before he ever mounts a horse and keeps a phial of holy water by his bed. He doesn't know if he's a Catholic or a Mussulman! I think he'll be whatever suits him.' Lumisden was angry.

Henry patted his arm and said soothingly, 'Take me to him now and I'll try to talk some sense into him.'

The brothers had not seen each other for twenty-one years and when Henry was shown into his brother's chamber, he faltered in surprise on the threshold for the man staring across at him bore no resemblance to the brother he remembered.

In 1745 his brother Charles had been elegantly thin, fair-haired, fresh-faced and humorous-looking with the pleasantly curving mouth that both brothers had inherited from their Polish mother.

The person looking at him now was a complete stranger – fat, flushed and petulant-looking as well as being slightly seedy though he was gorgeously dressed in satin breeches, a heavily embroidered surcoat and a newly powdered wig. The eyes that had once been sparkling and blue were sunk under swollen lids and underlined by deep purple bags; the cheeks were so criss-crossed with broken veins that it looked as if he was in a permanent flush; his belly hung down above spindly legs and the hands he held out in greeting to his brother visibly shook.

'Isn't this a terrible place? I don't know how I will be able to live in it. I hope I've been left enough money to do it up prop-erly. You look old, Brother, and you've become the typical churchman! But no monastic robes I see,' Charles exclaimed, for Henry was wearing a floor-length red robe with a heavy golden cross round his neck.

The remark about him looking old stung Henry, who knew that of the two of them Charles looked at least fifteen years older though there was only five years between them. Henry was taller and still spare. He was more swarthy skinned than Charles but that made him more of a Stewart because many of their fore-bears had been dark in complexion, with long noses and sharp, watchful eyes. Henry also looked clever and learned, which he was and which Charles definitely was not.

'It was a pity you couldn't arrive in time for our father's funeral. It was a High Mass conducted by the Pope himself which would have made you proud to see him treated with so much respect,' said Henry, angry that Charles had expressed not a word of regret about their father's passing.

'He deserved to be respected. He was King of England, Scotland, Ireland and Wales after all. As I am now too by rights. That's why I want the Pope to acknowledge me as Charles III. It sounds good, doesn't it? You must arrange an audience between us,' said Charles blithely.

'If you do meet the Pope I hope you behave better than you did when you were a boy and refused to kneel in front of him because you were a Prince and he was only an elected prelate,' Henry reminded him.

Charles laughed, unabashed. 'I've always been proud and outspoken, I'm afraid. Organize the audience for as soon as possible – today perhaps?'

In spite of what Lumisden said, Henry suspected that his brother had already been drinking. 'Even for Cardinals, organizing a meeting with the Pope takes time, I'm afraid. Also he might be doubtful about receiving you because of your commitment to the Protestant religion,' he said. He knew that there was no way a Pope would grant an official audience to a royal pretender who was Catholic one moment and Protestant the next.

Charles waved an airy hand. 'Tell him I'm still a true believer. I only joined the English church in London to win the Jacobites there over to my side. They didn't want to see another Catholic on the throne. It's their own fault that now they've got a bunch of Germans, half of which can't even speak English, ruling over them. The one on the throne now is said to have raving fits. When I make my next attempt to win back our throne, there'll be a very different outcome if I adopt the Protestant faith,' was his brother's reply and Henry suppressed a groan. Not only was Charles requesting an audience with the Pope but he was back on his old hobby horse of reclaiming the throne by invasion.

'The day for invasions and rebellions has passed I'm afraid,' he said firmly and Charles looked at him in surprise.

'Nonsense,' he said nastily. 'Why should it be over? Do you think I'm too old? I'm only forty-six and as fit as a twenty-five-year-old. I could still tramp over miles of heather if I had to. You don't look too fit to me. You're as thin as a rail and I'm sure your knees crack every time you kneel down to pray, if you ever do.'

Henry took the easy way out and decided to be conciliatory. 'All right, I'll ask the Pope to see you, but if he does, please do not bring up the subject of another invasion. He's very much against that idea and so is the King of France.'

'France comes and goes like the wind. Any time he wants to annoy the English he backs me up quickly enough.'

'I beg you to let the subject lie for the meantime,' said Henry diplomatically and started telling his brother how much money their father had left, which made Charles literally rub his hands in delight.

'A rich man at last,' he cried, knowing that for him there would be no more pleading for money from his tight-fisted father or anyone and everyone who came within his orbit; no more going cap in hand to the King of France and being told to go away and stay away whenever the King's patience wore thin.

'I knew the old devil had plenty and that's what annoyed me so much when he refused to let me have any of it,' he said in delight. He was already planning to launch himself on a great spending spree, and buy clothes, telescopes, more microscopes (like the one he never used) and jewels, as well as completely refurbishing the Palazzo.

One disadvantage of suddenly becoming rich, he quickly discovered, was that people from whom he had borrowed money started asking for it back, requests he found easy to ignore. He also managed to stifle his conscience and turn a blind eye when reminders came from people to whom he had promised payments or rewards for saving him in Scotland.

Flora Macdonald was not among the petitioners. She had assessed his character well enough to know that though he promised much, it was unlikely that he would ever fulfil any of his promises.

Henry stalled as long as he could over the Papal audience but eventually his persistence won through and the Pope agreed to allow Charles to accompany his brother into an audience, but he was determined to pay him no honour. It was the best Henry could manage and he had to bite his lip when Charles went off into speculations about what he would say to the Pope and how he expected the Pope to pay great honour to him. On the appointed day Henry turned up to collect Charles in his fine coach, a massive, gilded affair with the arms of Frascati on the sides and drawn by four black horses. The grandeur of this get-up delighted his brother who climbed in and settled himself in the corner seat with an unencumbered view out of the side window.

As they rolled through the streets of Rome, people turned to stare and bow at the coach as it passed and Charles leaned forward to exclaim to Henry, 'Look at how those people are waving at me. They know who I am and they're paying their respects.'

He spent the rest of the journey waving royally to the crowds on the roadways, totally unaware that the respect they were showing was for his brother, the Cardinal of Frascati, and not for him because as far as the Romans were concerned, he was a complete nonentity.

Realization began to dawn at the entrance to the Pope's receiving chamber when the major domo announced them only as 'His Grace the Cardinal of Frascati and his brother.' He looked outraged at not being named and was about to protest when Henry urged him forward and whispered that he should hold his tongue.

Worse was to follow. Inside the chamber the austere-looking Pope did not even invite Charles to sit down, though he was cordial but brief with Henry. They were out in the hall again within five minutes with no words having been directly addressed to Charles and no invitation extended to come again. On the return journey he sulked without waving to any more curious bystanders.

'I was right not to kneel to a Pope when I was a boy. That one we've just seen is a nobody with no breeding,' he said when he came out of his ill temper and agreed to speak again.

What followed were months of utter boredom for both brothers. Charles was out of temper because he was shunned both by the

Pope and by society and Henry was bored having to sit and listen to his drunken brother telling and retelling stories about his Highland adventures.

Henry wondered if he even knew that the boatmen who rowed him off Skye were all executed by the English, and that one thousand others who gave him assistance were deported to the southern states of America as slaves and never saw their homeland again, not to mention the men who died at Culloden, or lost their homes and their families while he sailed away in a French ship without a backward glance.

All the old Jacobite retainers who had clustered round James were arbitrarily sent away and replaced by Charles with Italians who blatantly stole from him and encouraged his drinking.

Because he had given Henry a promise to stay as long as possible, the secretary Lumisden hung on till the day he was ordered by Charles to drive him out though he was incapable through drink and the front of his clothes were marked with vomit.

'I will not go out with him when he looks like that,' Lumisden said and resigned on the spot though he had served the family for over forty years. Henry made sure he received a pension but no thought of such a thing for him or any of the other loyal retainers who had been dismissed ever crossed Charles' mind.

The situation in the Palazzo Muti was becoming intolerable when Henry's lover came up with an idea. If a distraction could be provided for his brother, at least Henry would not have to see him so often. Cesarini suggested, 'Why not marry him off?'

Before that subject could be broached with Charles however, it was necessary for Henry to make sure that his brother was never married to Clementine Walkinshaw because some people said that he had been. He sought out Lumisden, who was still in Rome, and said, 'I have one last thing I want you to do for our family, Andrew. I want you to go to Mrs Walkinshaw and ask her to write a solemn affidavit affirming that she and my brother were never legally married.'

Lumisden had always felt pity for the woman who'd lived so long and suffered so much with Charles. He agreed to go and made the long trip to France wondering how he was to phrase his request. Fortunately Clementine grasped his purpose quickly and asked directly, 'You've obviously come here on some specific errand. What exactly do you want from me?'

'I want you to sign a document saying you were never married to Charles Edward Stewart.'

She stared at him for a few moments before she asked, 'Is he planning to marry? Are you afraid I might accuse him of bigamy?'

'No, it's his brother Henry who wants the statement. He is trying to arrange a marriage for the Prince, who doesn't know anything about it yet,' Lumisden told her.

She stared into his face, trying to work out if he was sympathetic to her or not and then she asked, 'Will this in any way affect my daughter?'

He shook his head. 'I don't think so. Prince Charles never officially acknowledged her as his child, did he?'

'No, but she is his. She even resembles him.'

'I believe what you say is true. However his brother is anxious to preserve the Stewart line, and for that the Prince needs a legitimate heir. To do that he must marry. It will be difficult to find him a bride if he is even suspected of bigamy.'

Clementine nodded. She was a realistic woman who knew she could hold the Stewarts to ransom but she stared at him with clear honest eyes and said, 'I will not lie to you. I would have married him if he asked me but he never did and so we never underwent a marriage ceremony. He did not want me. He probably does not want any woman if the truth be told.'

'Will you write a document saying that?' asked Lumisden gently, trying to hide his relief at her probity.

'Come back tomorrow and I will have written what you require,' she told him.

Next day he was once more on his way back to Rome with a one-page document which stated categorically that Clementine Walkinshaw knew there were rumours that she had married Charles, once Prince of Wales, and presently King Charles III of Great Britain, but she swore before God that these rumours were untrue.

'I have never given the least room, either by word or writing, to such a falsehood,' she wrote and signed it with the place and date, March 9th 1767.

★   ★   ★

Once the document was safe in his hands, Henry said, 'Poor soul. She is a better woman than he deserved.' Now it was time for him to move.

'I think it's time you got married,' he said to Charles one cold spring day when he was being forced to listen to tales of heroism again.

'I've no wish to marry. I've had enough of women. Pederasts like you can have no idea how much trouble and annoyance they cause a man. If I need a woman, which isn't often, I can send out a servant to fetch me one off the street.'

Henry's face showed distaste and Charles rounded on him. 'At least it's natural. Not like you and your secretary.'

'But it's your duty to have a child to carry on the line.'

'You haven't done that, even though your child could also stake a claim to the throne.'

'But you're the heir.'

'I have a child already.'

'A girl that you've never acknowledged as yours,' said Henry coldly.

The accusation of letting the Stewart line die out was too much for Charles. 'Then if you feel so strongly about it you must be my pandar and find me a bride,' he sneered.

Ten

It took time for the Macdonalds to gather enough money for their passages to America and when they'd built up a small fund, Flora went down to Edinburgh to buy some of the necessities they wanted for their new life.

On her return it struck her that whenever she got back into the little boat that carried her off the mainland again her heart rose with love for her native country. She felt as if she was a deep-rooted plant that should not be uprooted from the place where she and all her ancestors had lived since time began.

Though she always enjoyed her short forays away she knew that life in London or Edinburgh was not for her. After a few days she always began to dream about the Highlands and longed to be back there. *How am I going to survive in another country with no way of getting home again?* she wondered and remembered the deep despair she felt during her year-long sojourn in the Tower of London in 1746.

But then she had been comforted by the hope that she might get out and go home again soon. In faraway America there would be no way out. Once she crossed the Atlantic, Skye would only be a memory.

Allan was waiting for her at their own landing stage when the boatmen rowed her home. He held out his hand to pull her ashore and grinned broadly. 'It's good you got home in time. Your fame has spread up from London again, my dear. Tomorrow we are going to have two very important visitors, young gallants who want to meet the famous Flora Macdonald.'

From time to time curious callers would occasionally turn up at Kingsburgh and ask to speak to Flora. They always stared at her for a bit and then bombarded her with questions about the Prince. She knew that their curiosity was because some people still believed that she helped Charles because she was in love with him, and even that they were lovers, but she always took care to dispel these misapprehensions though she knew that her visitors preferred the other version. It was more romantic.

'Who are they?' she asked because Allan seemed so pleased about these visitors. Normally he stayed out of the way when Jacobite worshippers arrived to talk to Flora.

'Two gentlemen apparently. One is a famous literary man from London and the other an advocate from Edinburgh, the son of Lord Auchinleck, the high court judge. We'll have to open the last of the claret for them and I've killed a lamb for their supper.'

Flora sighed and said, 'I'm sorry we're being bothered at this moment. We haven't had any Jacobite callers for quite a while, have we? Perhaps they'll travel on quickly when they see how ordinary I am.'

Allan bent and kissed her cheek. 'You're far from ordinary, my dear. I'm proud that people still want to come and see you. Let's go home now because it's going to rain again soon. They tell me the weather is better in Carolina.' He could not imagine that even he would one day long for the touch and taste of the drifting soft rain of Skye.

The next day was a wet Sunday in September and a soaking Dr Samuel Johnson and his younger companion James Boswell rode into Kingsburgh's yard. They'd only travelled a mile, or so their previous host said, but it was a Skye mile that seemed to go on and on till they were soaked to the skin and Johnson was very disgruntled. The novelty of his journey in the Highlands was beginning to wear off for him and he longed for his own London home, his caring black manservant Francis Barber and his cat Hodge.

Allan was waiting in the doorway for them and hustled them in to sit by a blazing fire which made steam rise from their clothes as they warmed up. Chrissie the maid bustled about draping blankets over their shoulders and taking away their wet boots. When she went into the kitchen where Flora was roasting meat, she said, 'Who told you they were a pair of young bucks? One's an ugly old fellow in his seventies and the other's a plump, black-haired fellow who fusses around the old man all the time.'

'Someone told Allan they were bucks. They must have been joking,' said Flora who hustled about because they had cut down their household staff so much that she now did all her own cooking and she hoped that Allan would entertain the guests till she had everything ready. In fact he managed very well, plying the guests with alcohol and charm. The whisky with which he filled their glasses helped to warm them up and soothed Johnson's bad temper.

It took half an hour before Flora appeared, flushed from the kitchen work but dressed in her best gown which sharp-eyed Boswell recognized from the reproductions of her portrait that had been issued when she returned from England in 1747.

As she walked into the room, a mountainous old man sitting by the fire stood up and graciously took her hand to kiss.

'I am pleased to meet a woman of such great bravery,' he said in a deep rumbling voice. She was surprised by the look of him because he was one of the ugliest men she had ever seen, with an enormous head made larger by a full-bottomed wig and a face that was deeply scarred by the marks of scrofula. His body was bulky too and his stomach hung down between his knees like a bladder but his courtesy and charm made her overlook his physical deficiencies.

She shook her head. 'Oh no, I wasn't brave. I just did what I had to do and it's all so long ago that I'm surprised anyone remembers about it.'

The younger of the travellers had also stood up and chimed in courteously, 'How can it be forgotten in Scotland! We have come here specially to talk to you. I'm from Edinburgh and my friend here is Dr Johnson of London, the author of the famous dictionary.' James Boswell was determined to draw out this shy little woman as much as possible – his advocate's training would come in useful there – and knew he must not drink too much because it was essential that he remember everything she said so he could write it up in the journal he was keeping of his travels with Dr Johnson.

She smiled at him and noticed that he had dancing dark eyes in a cherubic face. She decided that here was a kind, likeable man who was much more intelligent than he liked to pretend. His older companion was kind too but weary and in need of a good meal so she led him to the table and said, 'Please sit down and share our food. You have had a tiring journey. We can talk later.'

Samuel Johnson always responded well to charming women and he beamed at Flora, his wrinkled, scabrous face breaking into a smile that delighted her.

As they ate James Boswell was anxious to start on the subject that brought them to Kingsburgh. He told her, 'Dr Johnson and I were anxious to come to meet you because we want to hear all the details of how you saved the life of the grandson of King James II.'

It amused her that he used this roundabout way of referring to Prince Charles Edward Stewart. He was too honest to make her think that either he or Dr Johnson were Jacobites but would not want to call Charles 'The Young Pretender' in case she was one of his faithful followers who might resent the implication that he *pretended* to a throne.

'I think it is all right to call him Prince Charles Edward, because after all he was a descendant of the Kings of Poland, wasn't he?' she said jokingly and they all laughed. Her light-heartedness opened the floodgates of their conversation and both during the meal and after it the visitors besieged Flora with a stream of questions that brought back memories which she thought she had forgotten long ago.

'Tell us about the first time you saw him,' Boswell said and she nodded slowly, casting back through the years. 'I was asleep when a man came knocking at the cottage door to wake me up. He had a letter from my stepfather Hugh.' She recalled reading the letter by the light of a fading fire and shaking her head. 'Oh no, I can't do that,' she'd said.

'There's no one else to help us and the redcoats won't expect him to be travelling with a woman,' pleaded the messenger.

'But what if we're caught? There's a reward out for his capture and a lot of people will be looking out for him. Go away and leave me in peace,' she said, throwing Hugh's letter on to the floor.

At that moment the cottage door opened and he came in. Elegant even when ragged and very handsome, he looked every inch a prince even though his clothes were filthy and his boots broken. What struck her most forcibly was the fine curled wig that hung from his hand. Fleas were hopping off it and scuttling away across the cottage floor. *What a state for a prince to get into,* she'd thought.

'Please help me. You are the only one who can,' he said and his voice was charming with foreign intonations as if he was not used to speaking English.

'So you changed your mind then. Why?' asked Boswell.

'People always ask me that. The Prince of Wales and the Duke of Cumberland both asked the same question when I was imprisoned in London. All I can say is that he wakened my sympathy. I could not refuse to help a fellow human being in such dire straits. If Cumberland's men got him I knew they'd slay him like a dog and I couldn't let that happen.'

'So you dressed him up as a woman and passed him off as your maid,' Johnson said and laughed. She laughed too, remembering the awkward Betty Burke. 'Yes. I pretended I was going to visit my mother on Skye so we crossed from Raasay to Kingsburgh here and it took us two days to stitch him a gown. When he got away at the end my mother-in-law made a quilt out of his skirts. It's still on the bed you'll sleep in tonight,' she told him.

'Did you keep any souvenirs of him?' asked Boswell and she shook her head.

'Not really. I was too concerned with getting him across the island in safety. My mother-in-law cut off a lock of his hair when he was asleep and gave me some of it but I lost it later. She was buried in his bed sheet which she never washed after he slept in it. She was a very faithful Jacobite.'

'You guided him for twelve days, didn't you? And there were English soldiers looking for you everywhere. Weren't you afraid that you'd be caught?' Johnson asked her.

'I don't remember being afraid but I did get anxious at times when he insisted on singing Jacobite songs very loudly as we walked along.' She remembered trying to hush the Prince as he belted out 'The King Shall Have His Own Again'.

Boswell laughed when she told them that and she went on to add, 'I went from day to day and trusted that any local people who saw us would look the other way and ask no questions. I was too busy to be afraid.'

'Did he reward you?' Johnson asked softly.

'I expected no reward. I did what I was asked to do and passed him on to his next escort.'

'Have you ever heard from him since?'

'No.' She remembered seeing him in the Strand and how angry she felt because of all the people who'd suffered on his behalf, but she did not want to talk about that.

'Did you like him?' It was the old man asking the question again and she felt as if he was able to see inside her mind.

'He was not used to taking orders, especially from a woman. It was difficult for him to do as he was told, but then he was a prince and princes are different, aren't they? He was always very jovial . . .' Her voice trailed off.

She was not going to tell them about his continual drinking. One of their fugitive party was burdened with the bottles of brandy he drank – two a day at least – and somehow or other his female supporters managed to get them to him though they would never have risked their lives by doing what Flora undertook.

'You are a real heroine and I am very honoured to have met you,' said Dr Johnson, rising stiffly to his feet and kissing her hand. Then he said he was very tired and wanted to go to bed.

Boswell and Allan helped him upstairs and into the same bed that Charles had slept in. He slept deeply and woke refreshed to lie for a while watching dawn streaking the sky and pondering everything he heard the night before. Charles Edward Stewart was not a very nice or grateful man, he decided, but then, as Flora said, perhaps princes are different and should be excused their lack of gratitude or remorse.

At the breakfast table he said to a bustling Flora, 'I've never slept in a Prince's bed before and I found it very comfortable, but it's time to get on the road again. I'm missing the city, I think.'

She smiled at him and replied, 'And I miss the mountains when I'm in the city so I know what you mean.'

Johnson and Boswell were ferried off Skye by Allan who dressed himself up specially for the occasion and stood proudly in the prow of the boat with his plaid over his shoulder, his hair tied back in a queue, a blue bonnet with black riband and cockade and a short brown coat with golden buttons and golden stitched buttonholes. He looked like a magnate and no one could have guessed that he was on the verge of penury.

Johnson had heard from other people on Skye that Allan and

Flora were about to sail for America in an effort to turn their fortunes round and he regarded his host with a sad but sympathetic eye and sincerely hoped that emigration would be the right move for them.

As their little boat cut through the water, he leaned across to Allan and said, 'You have a very fine wife, sir.'

'Indeed I know it,' said Allan proudly.

'Before I left your house I wrote a little note and left it on the Prince's bed. Tell her it is for her, will you please?' said the old man.

When he returned Allan ran upstairs and brought down a folded piece of paper which he gave to Flora and said, 'Dr Johnson told me he'd left this note for you.'

He had not read it himself so she unfolded it and puzzled over the words. 'I can't understand it,' she said and passed the note back to Allan.

'It's in Latin. I studied Latin at school. Let's see if I can remember any of it. It says *Quantum cedat virtutibus aurum.* Virtutibus is goodness or virtue, yes, I've got it. He's written "With virtue weighed what worthless trash is gold". He told me to say he wrote it for you. He's valuing you above gold and he's quite correct.' Then he held out his arms and she walked into his embrace, full of love.

It took another year before they were ready to leave and during that time Flora had the problem of trying to settle her children. James was the only one of the boys who really wanted to go to America. Ranald, who was seventeen, found a position as a lieutenant in the marines and John, the most clever of the family, was studying at Edinburgh's High School and doing well, so he did not want to leave. Lodgings were found for him in the capital with the kind and forgiving Mr Mackenzie, so the number of passages to be booked dwindled to Allan and Flora, James and little Fanny who was eight and none too strong.

Like John she did not want to go to America and wept every time her mother talked about it. 'I don't want to leave home,' she said over and over again. Flora looked at the sobbing child with sympathy. *I don't want to go either*, she thought but knew she must not say so. Go she must, like it or not.

'But when we go you can't stay here alone,' she said, holding Fanny in her arms.

'Let me stay here on Skye with Anne,' said Fanny looking up into her mother's face.

'I'll ask her what she thinks,' said Flora but when she suggested Fanny's idea, Anne's face clouded. 'Oh, Mother, I would have taken her with pleasure but my husband is so fired up about your plans of going to Carolina that he's talking of going too and has been to Portree enquiring about passages for us and the babies. We'll be following you but I didn't want to tell you before it was all finalized.'

Flora gasped, half delighted that she was not going to lose her eldest daughter and the two small granddaughters that Anne had already given her, and half agonized about what to do with Fanny who had taken to running away and hiding in one of the barns whenever the conversation turned to Carolina.

'It's good that you are coming with us, but what about Fanny?' she asked her daughter.

'I know how miserable she is about going away from here and I've been asking people if they would take her. My grandmother didn't want the responsibility but my husband's half-sister lives on Raasay and she has ten daughters of her own already. I'm sure she'll take Fanny and bring her up well.'

'I knew my mother wouldn't want her and I don't think I'd like to leave her there,' said Flora because Marion had been a hard-hearted mother to her when she was small, leaving her for most of the time with her brother and two old aunts on Raasay.

'Bring her to meet Macleod's sister Charlotte and we can see what she thinks of my idea,' said Anne.

The meeting went well and all the women liked each other. Charlotte embraced Fanny and Flora when they met and held Flora's hand as she promised, 'I will love your little girl, I promise, and do my best for her. I love children and have got very used to having them around but my youngest is growing up now and she'll probably be getting married soon so it will be good for me to have another.'

'My heart is sore at the thought of leaving my baby,' said Flora.

'My dear, take courage. Going to America is not a life sentence. People come back, you know. When things go well there, you'll be able to return home and see your Fanny again. All you have to do is believe that it is possible and I'll take the greatest care of your girl in the meantime. I promise you that.'

Everyone wept on the day of parting. Even Allan had to wipe his eyes on the end of his plaid when he said goodbye to Fanny. Flora sailed to Raasay with her and fussed like a mother hen when they arrived at Charlotte's big house.

'She's so thin, and she can get a bad cough in the winter time. I always wrap her chest in flannel . . .'

She kept talking till Charlotte grasped her hands and said, 'Please be calm. I'll feed her up on curds and cream so you won't be able to recognize her when you come back. She'll write to you every week and I'll make sure she is happy. Go now before the tide turns and rest assured that she is safe with me.'

These reassurances however did not prevent Flora sobbing as if her heart was breaking when she was being rowed home.

The last days at Kingsburgh were chaotic. Boxes and trunks had to be packed, unpacked and repacked. Furniture that was too bulky to freight abroad was farmed out to various friends and relations, with the proviso it would be reclaimed if they returned. The Prince's bed went to a cousin of Allan who was not over impressed by its history because he was not a Jacobite supporter having lost his father and two brothers at Culloden.

On the July day that Allan, his wife and son James set sail from Campbeltown, the sun was blazing down and the islands looked magnificent, floating in an azure sea. Flora saw nothing of the landscape because her eyes were brimming with tears.

Allan put his arm around her and hugged her to his side, saying, 'I'll bring you back. I promise I'll bring you back.'

She nodded without speaking. He would bring her back, she was sure. He was her man and she trusted him.

Because they tried to spend as little money as possible on their passages, they all travelled in a small cramped cabin that provided no space for relaxing. The voyage lasted six weeks and by the end of it, the food was maggoty and foul tasting.

On the morning that the outline of land appeared on the horizon, Allan and Flora stood on deck and gazed at it as if it was the Promised Land. He, as usual, was ebullient and hopeful and she smiled up at him, pleased by his enthusiasm.

The captain was passing and Allan stopped him to ask, 'When do we reach land?'

'We dock in New Brunswick tonight. You'll be on land by midnight.'

Allan pointed out at the misty headland and asked, 'Is that New Brunswick?'

'No,' said the captain. 'That's called Cape Fear.'

Eleven

1776

Flora stood on deck with her elbows on the rail, staring out at this new land, America. Wryly she remembered the many times she and Allan had danced a dance called America at ceilidhs at home. In the dance couples fell out one by one till no one was left on the floor. It was the dance of the Scottish exodus and now she was one of the dancers who was being whirled away.

Tears filled her eyes but she quickly wiped them for she did not want Allan to see how upset she was. He was in high spirits, plaid proudly over his shoulder, standing tall in the prow with his son James beside him, both of them eager to challenge and dominate this new place.

'I miss my home. I miss my children. I miss the islands. I miss the hills of Skye and the view across the sound to Raasay,' she thought miserably and not for the first time wondered how her life would have gone if she had never woken up in the hut and seen Prince Charles Edward Stewart standing in front of her and asking for her help.

The twelve days they spent together changed her destiny because without her fame and her dowry she could never have aspired to a marriage with Allan MacDonald. Her husband would just have been a small tacksman probably . . . She drove those thoughts away.

'I've been very lucky. I love my husband and my children. I must face this challenge in the same way as I've faced challenges in the past,' she told herself and gathering her shawl round her she smiled and walked towards her men, calling out, 'Let's go ashore! I want to see this new place.'

Allan was not an imaginative man, but he had been worried in case his wife would miss her home and her other children too much. Seeing her smile, he whooped and swept her off her feet in a huge embrace and called out, 'And this new place America must meet the famous Flora Macdonald.' His pride in her was immense and he never stopped boasting that she was the saviour of the Stewart Prince even though that often won her as many enemies as friends.

'Oh hush, Allan, hush,' she pleaded as they made their way along the dock and Allan insisted on telling strangers who she was. Most of them were either unimpressed or disdainful. Many had come to America to escape the fiasco of the '45 and did not want to be reminded of it.

'Where are ye bound for?' one kindly faced old man asked Allan, who said that they had found a house and some land at North Carolina because he knew that a lot of Scottish people had settled there.

The man nodded and asked, 'That's a big stretch. Where exactly?'

'On the border of Virginia. A place called Mount Vernon.'

The stranger laughed. 'You're going right into Patriot country then.'

'Patriot country? Do you mean Jacobite? I came because I was told a lot of Scots have settled there.'

'I mean American patriots. Mount Vernon is Washington's place. He's none too fond of the English at the moment but the Scots might be all right with him.'

'We're Scots. My wife here saved the life of the Young Chevalier, and the English weren't very fond of him either.'

The stranger shrugged. 'Whoever he is. Well the best of luck anyway. This is a great country for people who aren't afraid to work. He looked at Flora with a pitying eye as if summing up her potential as an outback woman and finding her wanting.

Mount Vernon was set in soft luscious country with thick plan-tations of trees and fields full of an unfamiliar large-leafed crop that was browning in the last of the autumn sun. Flora was surprised to see that the people reaping the large stalks were all black and some wore iron braces like dogs' collars round their necks. White men with whips were overseeing them as they laboured.

She turned in her saddle and asked Allan, 'Who are these people?' In London on one or two occasions she had seen a blackamoor servant in livery but she had never seen so many black people all working together.

Allan had been picking up information on their two days' travel from the ship and said, 'They'll be George Washington's slaves. He grows tobacco here.'

'Slaves?' Her tone of voice showed her surprise and she was gripped by the memory of islanders from home who she knew had been transported as slaves to America as a punishment for supporting Charlie.

'I'll buy some for us as soon as we're settled. You'll need women in the house and I need some men for our farm if we're to grow enough crops to breed cattle,' said Allan.

'I don't want any slaves,' she replied firmly.

He laughed. 'We can't do everything ourselves. Our neighbours will tell us where to buy the best and how to treat them.' It was as if he was talking about the cattle that he hoped to breed in this strange land.

Typically Allan had taken the plunge of settling for North Carolina because people he knew in Edinburgh said many Scots had gone there and prospered. The trouble was that most of them were Lowlanders who were wary about people from the islands, and especially of Flora when Allan kept on telling them of her adventures with Bonnie Prince Charlie.

Lowlanders were not Jacobites and they thought of the '45 as a quixotic, disastrous folly. If Flora had any sense, they reckoned, she should have turned him in to the redcoats and taken the reward.

There was no hospitable welcome for new arrivals in Carolina like there would have been on Skye. The Macdonalds, and Anne with her husband Macleod and their small children who arrived soon after Allan and Flora, were treated with courtesy but left to get on with their lives as well as they could. This was not ceilidh country and if people celebrated with parties and drinking, they did so in privacy with close friends.

The winter was bitter with drifting snow that horrified Flora because it seemed to seep underneath the frames of the doors and windows like insidious fingers. Her bones hurt and even when spring came she found the lushness of the vegetation and close proximity of so many trees suffocating. She was used to emptiness, to long views over seas to shadowy islands.

Mount Vernon suffocated her and she felt very alien among the people.

The most respected man in the district was George Washington, a member of a long-established family who sat in the House of Burgesses for Virginia and was treated with high respect in the district. He and Allan spoke in passing a few times and Allan came home round-eyed to tell Flora, 'That Washington man has the most extraordinary teeth I've ever seen. I swear they're made of wood!'

'Can he speak properly?' she asked in surprise.

Allan said, 'Not only properly but very fluently. Apparently he's a great orator in the political assembly.'

'We've had enough of politics to last us for the rest of our lives,' said Flora shortly, hoping that Allan had no ambitions to get embroiled on his own behalf for very soon after they settled in their new home they found they were in the middle of a political ferment.

George Washington, who she often saw in the distance but never actually met, stood an impressive six feet four inches tall and towered over his followers, all of whom were vehemently opposed to the British government which levied heavy taxes on them and everything they did. They wanted to be able to rule and tax themselves.

Within months of arriving in Mount Vernon, Allan and Flora heard that George Washington had been elected Commander in Chief of the Continental Army to fight against British rule.

She wrung her hands when she heard this news and said in anguish, 'My God, we've only just escaped from a war at home and now we've landed in the middle of another one.'

Allan was not so distraught. 'These Patriots as they call themselves will not get anywhere. The British rule is too strong. They're only squabbling about money and have to be brought to heel like naughty children. Don't worry, my dear, no war will touch us here. We'll make our position obvious and line up with the established government.'

'With the Hanoverians?' she asked and Allan nodded.

'Indeed with the Hanoverians. I was an officer in the Hanoverian army in Forty-Five after all.'

But I went with the Jacobites, she thought, and then remembered that Allan's side won.

So why do I feel that this is the wrong thing to do? she wondered. She normally went along with anything her husband did – and although most of his affairs went wrong that was never his fault. This time however she was convinced from the beginning that he was taking the wrong course.

For several months there was no sighting of the immensely tall Washington on his farmlands but his wife Martha bustled about as usual, directing affairs. Like her husband she was polite to the newcomers but extended no open hospitality.

Then, when news came that Washington's army was harrying British garrisons all over the region, Allan took the plunge and signed on as Lieutenant Colonel and second in command of the Regiment of Scottish Highlanders which was incongruously loyal to the Hanoverian side and the only body of men in Carolina to take up that position. By this time Ranald had joined them and his two sons and his son-in-law, Anne's husband, joined up with him.

When Flora heard that her sons were taking to the field with their father, she wept and berated him, saying, 'You're taking away all the men of this family. You're even taking Anne's man to war with you. How do you expect us to survive here without them?'

He held her in his arms and reassured her. 'We won't be gone long and our friends here will look after you. These Colonists are disorganized and can never hold out long against the British forces. When we come back, we'll be in a stronger position than ever. We'll be on the winning side.'

Flora's fears were softened temporarily but she should have remembered her husband's unfortunate habit of always erring on the side of starry-eyed optimism.

The men set off on a bright May morning. Allan looked as handsome as ever in the red coat he'd worn in '45 and Anne's husband had his old Hanoverian uniform as well. Flora and her daughter made two new red coats for Ranald and Alexander. Watched by Anne's frightened children, the women clung together in tears as the handsome quartet disappeared up the long track to Boston.

The next month was a time of torment. Every time a rider came into view Flora rushed to the door and stood with her hands clasped in front of her apron and her eyes staring.

The few slaves that she and Allan had been able to afford had no reason to support her because a win for either side would do nothing for their situation, but Allan was a reasonable, kindly man who did not practise the cruelties on his workforce that some white men did so they were not openly hostile.

As the weather grew warmer, a Negro woman called Bessie, who had taken Chrissie's place in looking after Flora, brought her long cool drinks when she looked particularly distraught.

News was hard to come by, often shouted by a horseman galloping past, so she heard from time to time that all her men were well and still together.

Surprisingly the slaves seemed to hear news more quickly than any of the white families round about and on the late afternoon of June 18th it was from one of her labourers that Flora heard that a big battle was going on.

'Where is it?' she asked, wondering if her men were involved.

He was a powerful intelligent man in his mid forties who was highly respected among his work fellows. 'Near Boston, ma'am,' he told her and she shivered. The last she'd heard from Allan was that they were in Boston.

'Is it a big battle?'

'Very big. There are more redcoats than Colonists fighting round Breed's Hill and Bunker Hill.'

'Where's that?'

'On a point of land about two miles south-east of Boston.'

'Has it been going on long?'

'All day.'

'Who is winning?'

'First one and then the other. No one is sure yet.'

Because he saw how her face was quivering, and he liked the shy little woman, he did not add that there were many casualties on the Hanoverian side because the Colonists, all skilled snipers, found it easy to pinpoint men in scarlet coats.

'Please bring me any more news you hear,' she said and hurried inside to break the news to Anne.

Late at night, the son of one of their near neighbours who had also joined the Scottish Highlanders regiment came in the tatters of his torn, blood-stained uniform to tell Flora that Allan was dead.

As she always did when faced with real disaster, she summoned up self-will and kept her face expressionless as she asked, 'And my sons?'

'They're prisoners, I think.'

She thanked him for his courtesy in risking his own safety in Colonist country to bring her the news, but as soon as the door was closed behind him, she fell on to the floor in a fit of hysterics which terrified her daughter because she had never seen her mother give way to such an extent before.

On the following day Flora was lying in bed, semi-conscious and shuddering with fever, when their most unfriendly neighbour, a leather-jacketed Colonist with a hard-faced wife, drove up in a buggy and told Anne that Allan was not dead but had been taken prisoner, as had his sons.

The neighbours were triumphant in victory although it had been a pyrrhic one. While 225 British fighting men had been killed, the Colonists only lost 140 but had also roped in about 700 prisoners and were not prepared to let them out to start making trouble again, as the neighbour bluntly put it.

'And my husband? What's happened to him?' quavered Anne.

'Time will tell because I've no news. We're at war with the Hanoverians now, and as far as we're concerned, you're the enemy,' said the neighbour. Then he cracked his whip over the head of his horse and drove away.

Three days later he came back with three companions and was met by Anne at the front door.

'My mother is very unwell and can see no one,' she said sternly.

'She'll want to hear what I have to say. Allan Macdonald is alive and being held prisoner with his sons.'

'Held by who?'

'By the Patriot Committee of Safety.'

'And who are they?' asked the spirited Anne.

'We are!' The neighbour threw out his arm to indicate his grim-looking companions.

She slammed the door shut but he rapped on it with the butt of his gun.

'Tell your mother that her husband has been judged guilty of persuading men to join his Royal Highland Regiment and as penalty for this we are seizing his lands and destroying his crops,' he shouted before he left.

Anne stayed still for a long time with her back pressed against the inside of the door. She had always loved her father but from an early age she'd realized that he was prone to taking rash decisions and that the true mainstay of their family was her deceptively frail-looking mother. Slowly she walked through the house to where Flora lay in bed, huddled up like a child.

'Did you hear that?' she asked.

'Yes, thank God your father and the boys are alive but what about your man?'

'He wasn't mentioned.'

'God grant he is safe. He's a more seasoned campaigner than your father.'

'They've seized your lands and stock and will burn your crops.'

'I heard. If we have no stock to feed, it won't matter about the crop.'

'I'm afraid. I think we should leave here.'

'But what if your father comes back looking for me?' asked Flora.

'We should go to his Hanoverian friends in Boston.' Anne told her.

Flora pulled the sheet up over her face as she said, 'Let me think about this. You and the children can go to Boston but I'll stay here for the meantime.'

'I'm going nowhere without you,' said Anne stoutly.

They stayed embattled in the house for a week, living off the produce of their kitchen garden till one night they were alerted by a scratching sound at the window. Anne pulled back the curtain and saw a figure huddled by the wall. It was her husband.

'You've all got to come away with me at once. The Committee of Public Safety are out to ruin your mother because of Allan raising his regiment against the Colonists. Have you still got a horse?' he asked after they hugged each other in weeping relief.

'Yes, two.'

'And I have another. Get ready and we'll go to Boston. Leave everything behind. It doesn't matter.'

Because he was so determined Flora realized that she was indeed in danger and before midnight, when a sickle moon was swimming in the sky, the family slunk out of the house, and led their horses to a wood where they mounted, Anne and her husband each with a child behind them, and Flora riding on her own. They were in Boston, in the large house of a Hanoverian colleague of Allan's, by dawn.

For over a year Flora went in secret from one Loyalist household to another, always ill, always aching from rheumatism, always eagerly awaiting news from Allan which arrived from time to time and was invariably cheerful. He and the boys were well and as soon as they were free they would take the field again on behalf of King George. Then more word came too from Ranald who had escaped from imprisonment and enlisted on a ship of the British navy.

But the war between the supporters of the British government and the Colonists was not going the British way. They were forced to abandon Boston in 1776 and on July 4th of that year Thomas Jefferson read out the Declaration of Independence from Britain in Washington. Five days later George Washington read it to his army in New York City. Only starry-eyed optimists thought that British rule would prevail. Among them was Allan Macdonald and his son James who were released from captivity because there was little point keeping them cooped up any longer.

When Allan got back to Boston at last he and Flora clung to each other, both in floods of tears. He was as fit and handsome as ever but the change in her was a shock to him for she seemed to have aged twenty years in the two that had passed since they last saw each other.

'Oh Allan, what are we going to do? Anne's husband wants to take her back to Skye and she's only stayed here because of me, but she must go now. Will you go back to Mount Vernon and reclaim your land?'

'I'll try to get as much as possible for it but those people don't like me and they'll make sure they take it off me for as little as possible. But I've been offered the command of the New York Loyalists who are holding out against George Washington and his men.'

'Not against Washington again!' exclaimed Flora who associated that name with all their bad luck.

'I want to go on fighting and I want to take you with me because Boston has more or less gone over to the other side. We'll make a new start in New York, I'm sure of it.'

In her heart Flora knew this was just another of Allan's optimistic new beginnings but she loved him so she agreed to go.

They arrived in New York at the time of many defeats for the British, first at the battle of Trenton and then at Saratoga. They were soon on the move again, but this time Flora was happy to have both her husband and her sons Alexander and Ranald, who had turned up again and joined his father as an officer in the New York Loyalists.

Her men saw that she was ill but none of them knew what to do to help her. Then Allan heard that land was being granted out to Loyalists in Nova Scotia and, all beaming, told Flora about this new opportunity.

'Nova Scotia – New Scotland! People say it's beautiful, as beautiful as the Highlands. And the settlers are nearly all Highlanders like ourselves. The climate will suit you better than North Carolina as well. It was too hot and clammy for you there, I think,' he told her.

'It was. I felt tired all the time. It would be good to feel soft rain on my cheeks once more,' she said with a smile, but she was forcing herself. The place she wanted to go back to was Skye. They travelled north the following week.

Nova Scotia intimidated her because there were parts of it that were too reminiscent of her home. She grew thinner and paler and lost energy till it was a struggle for her to perform the smallest task and she was worried because Allan had become obsessed with claiming his rights and recovering money he said was due to him because of the confiscation of his land and possessions in Carolina.

When Flora pleaded with him to take her home to Scotland, he shook his head, and said, 'We can't go till we get our rights. I have to fight for what we've lost.'

Because her mother was staying, Anne had still not agreed to go back to Scotland though her husband pressed her to do so all the time. 'I can't leave my mother,' was all she said.

'Then she must come with us because we are going now,' was his firm reply.

Anne talked sense into her father. 'If my mother doesn't leave here she will die. She left her heart in Skye and her only chance of living again is to go back there. If you won't take her, I will,' she said.

Allan was deeply concerned because he had closed his eyes to Flora's uncomplaining misery. He agreed that his wife should accompany her daughter and family back to Skye and when they parted on the quayside of Halifax, they clung together like young lovers and wept.

'I'll be in Skye with you in a few months, as soon as I get my compensation, and then we'll set up in comfort again,' he promised her.

It was a long and uncomfortable voyage with high seas all the way. Shouting woke Flora early one morning in the middle of the ocean when they were only halfway home and she struggled out of her tiny bunk, dragged on her shawl and went on to the deck where she found some crew men running around trimming the sails while others were dragging out cannons.

The captain, with his red nightcap still on his head, was directing operations and she hurried up to ask him, 'What is happening, Captain Peacock?'

'Madam, please go back below deck. There's a Frenchman chasing us.'

'A Frenchman?' She looked around, incredulous.

'A French privateer. We're at war with them now, you know. They went in on the side of the Colonists. Go below please.'

She looked in the direction that he was staring and saw that a sharp-looking full-sailed ship was chasing along behind them. Puffs of smoke were coming from its cannons.

'We'll have to outrun them or they'll take my cargo and probably kill the lot of us. Go below!' he snapped.

By this time Anne had joined Flora on deck and she took her mother's arm. 'Let's do as the Captain says, Mother. We're only going to be in the way here,' she said, but Flora was reluctant and hung back, keen to share the excitement on deck. Anne was insistent and pulled at her mother's arm just as their own ship changed tack and dipped sharply to the right, throwing Flora off her feet. She hit the deck with her left elbow and felt the bone crumple beneath her.

Engulfed by waves of terrible pain, she groaned. 'I think my arm is broken, Anne.'

She was lifted and bundled into a cabin where she lay trying to stop herself from groaning in agony while the flight from the Frenchman went on.

Captain Peacock's seamanship proved superior and after an hour he outran his pursuer. Then, still wearing his nightcap, he went to check on Flora who was holding her arm tight against her body in an attempt to quell the pain. She could not lift it or clench her fist and he could see that the break was bad.

'There's a lad on board who says he's studying to be a doctor. I'll send him in to set the break for you,' he told her.

A boy who looked about sixteen was brought in a few minutes later and was obviously too overawed by the captain to admit to ignorance. 'This lady has a broken arm. Set it and put it in a sling for her,' he was ordered.

'I've never set an arm before,' protested the boy.

'You said you're a medical student, didn't you?' snapped Captain Peacock.

'I'm only in my first year.'

'Then this'll be good practice. Go and get your books to find out what to do and do it.'

Flora was rendered semi-conscious with brandy while the operation was done by the fumbling boy who was faced with a bigger task than any of them realized because the elbow had been smashed to pieces and could not be set properly.

Whenever Flora flinched, Anne held the brandy glass to her lips and after she took a very welcome sip she whispered, 'Now I know why the Prince needed his brandy every day. It's a wonderful comforter in bad times.'

When they reached London three weeks later, Flora's arm was hideously painful but she hid her agony because she knew it worried Anne, and also because they still had the long journey to the islands to undergo, and to them she must return.

But there was more sorrow to endure before she got there.

She was able to go to bed in the same inn as she had stayed when she was in London thirty years previously, in 1750, when a messenger with bad news came from Lady Margaret Macdonald who was also in London but still not prepared to forgive Flora for embroiling her in the Charlie debacle so would not come herself.

The man stood nervously crumpling his bonnet in his hands as he said, 'Mistress Macdonald, my lady has sent me to give you some news she has just received from America.'

She looked up at him with fear clearly showing in her face. 'What is it?' She knew it must be serious if her old enemy was taking the trouble to pass it on to her.

'I'm very sorry,' he mumbled.

She snapped, 'Tell me! Is it news of my husband?' She was terrified in case Allan was dead.

'No. I'm very sorry. It's your son.'

'Which son?'

'James. He was returning to England to join you here when his ship foundered and, I'm very sorry, but he was drowned.'

She gave a terrible groan and fainted.

There was more to come. A week later more news came of another drowning. This time it was Ranald, who had rejoined the navy. It was almost beyond belief and very hard to bear.

'The sea has taken my two boys,' mourned Flora and wished that she and Allan could have been together to bear this terrible burden but he was still trying to regain the value of the land he reckoned had been unlawfully taken away from him. Fuelled by indignation, he was once again fighting on the Hanoverian side in the war in America and there was no way she could contact him.

At last, through his rich Macleod connections, Anne's husband arranged for her to travel slowly north but by the time she saw Skye again it was 1780. Her stoical nature failed her when she once again looked out at the mist-crowned blue mountains.

'I'm home, thank God I'm home,' she sobbed and at last burst into terrible pent-up weeping.

There was a little consolation for her in the shape of a message from her son John who, after schooling, had followed his brother Charles to work in the East India Company and, being clever, had prospered. His loving letter was waiting for his mother when she returned to Skye and it included a money draft for a thousand pounds – 'to make your life more comfortable,' he wrote.

To the returned traveller it was a fortune and she stared at the draft in great relief. 'Bless him,' she said because she was by this time penniless and dependent on the charity of her son-in-law and brother who lived on Raasay in Milton, the house where she had been born.

One-Eyed Hugh and Marion were both dead, but Flora was anxious to be reunited with her youngest daughter Fanny who was still on Raasay and as soon as she was able she travelled to her brother's house for a reunion.

The baby she'd left had been a skinny little eight-year-old. The young woman who rushed into her arms at Milton was a plump stranger who had Allan's lovely dark hair and her mother's pale skin. It struck Flora that if she passed this girl on the road she would not have recognized her as one of her own. So long had passed, so much had happened.

Not unnaturally Fanny was more attached to her foster family than she was to the people who had sailed away to America and who she remembered only dimly. Before meeting her mother again, she had been warned by her kindly Macleod foster mother not to show surprise if she thought Flora much changed.

'She has been ill and is grieving for your two dead brothers. Make a fuss of her, tell her you love her and even if you hardly remember her, pretend that you do,' she was told.

Even with this advice ringing in her mind, Fanny hesitated when she entered the room and saw two women sitting by the fireside and staring at her. She was about to run up and embrace Anne, who did resemble the mother she remembered, when she was stopped short by the dreadful realization that the thin, grey-haired old woman with the crippled arm was the one she should be kissing. Flora saw the hesitation and her heart ached.

Fanny turned out to be a cheerful, chattering young woman, however, who soon bridged the gap with her mother and older sister by chattering about everything and anything that came into her mind. She told her mother, 'I'm going to stay here at Milton with you, Mother, and fatten you up. You're too thin. I want to get married soon and you'll have to be looking fit and well for my wedding.'

'Married? When?' Flora was astonished at this announcement from her baby.

'There's no date picked yet. Not for about a year yet. But I have my eye on my husband and I won't let him escape.'

'Who is he?' In Flora's day weddings were arranged between families, usually by the fathers of the bride and groom as hers had been, but she'd heard nothing of this.

'You'll like him. He's one of my cousins and his father's a big tacksman.'

'Which cousin? Is he from my family?' Allan had relatives all over Skye but no direct cousins as far as Flora knew.

Fanny paused in her prattling and said, 'Oh no, Mother, he's one of my Macleod cousins . . .' Her voice trailed off as she realized her mistake, but Flora showed no sign of being hurt though the significance of what her daughter said had not escaped her. She'd given her child away entirely when she went to America, it seemed.

Flora stayed on Raasay for almost a year and gradually regained some of her health. If the weather was fine and her arm did not hurt too much she and Fanny climbed a little hill behind the house and she sat staring out at sea, thinking about her dead sons lying beneath its waves and also remembering the night she saw the ragged young Prince standing before her with a lice-infested wig in his hand, asking her to help him.

What sort of life would I have had, what would have happened to me if I'd refused? she wondered. Then she looked at Fanny, who was always cheerful and full of life. Fanny, her sister and brothers would never have been born if she hadn't married Allan, and that would have been unlikely without the money she was given by Lady Primrose for saving Charlie.

After ten months Fanny wanted to go back to the Macleod household to organize her wedding, and Flora went to live with Anne at Dunvegan Castle on Skye where her husband had been appointed tutor to the sons of the head of his clan and they were living in considerable comfort.

Letters arrived in a regular stream from Allan. He wrote fluently and as she read them she could hear his voice speaking to her though they had been separated for five years.

After the American war ended, he was despondent but, being Allan, he recovered his optimism when he was granted a stretch of 3,000 acres of compensatory land in Nova Scotia to make up for the property taken from him at Mount Vernon.

He went back there and built a cabin, writing to Flora about buying stock and planting crops, but as winter engulfed the grim land he realized that he was growing old – for he was now sixty – and without his dead sons to help him, he was unable to make the place either liveable or profitable.

Flora's arm was still giving her much pain and she was half crippled with rheumatics, which the anxiety about Allan did not help. She began to think she would never see him again but her depression was lifted one morning when an excited Anne came rushing into her bedroom with a letter in her hand, exulting, 'Mother, Mother, here's good news. Father's coming home at last.'

Flora sat up in bed and cried out, 'Oh, thank God! When?'

'He's in London now. He's petitioning the government for compensation for being a loyal Hanoverian and backing the King in the Colonists' war.'

Flora groaned. Allan was off on another campaign. 'Why doesn't he just come home at once?' she groaned.

Anne laughed. 'You know what he's like. He's always got to have some campaign to wage.'

And he usually loses, thought Flora hopelessly.

For several months Allan's letters poured in – alternately elated and depressed. He thought that because he had raised a loyal regiment to fight for the King and lost everything, including two sons, he should be reimbursed with the sum of £1341. How this sum was estimated was neatly worked out and itemized but his request was thrown out three times.

Undeterred he kept on petitioning until he was finally offered £440, which he eventually accepted because he was told that if he didn't, he'd get nothing.

In 1784 Allan Macdonald at last returned to Dunvegan in Skye and his crippled wife. In spite of the rigours he had endured he was much less aged by their American adventures than she was.

Their reunion was like the meeting of lovers and they clung together, both in tears, crying about so many sad things, lost hopes, and lost children.

When they dried their tears, Allan told her, 'Cheer up, my dear. I'll set us up again.'

'Oh, please don't. I only want a quiet life now,' she implored him.

With financial help from John in India, who was turning into a nabob, Allan managed to rent a house at Penduin, near his parents' old home at Kingsburgh. He even managed to get his hands on some of their old furniture, including the bed in which the Prince had once slept.

He carried Flora over the threshold, feeling shock at how little she weighed nowadays, and laid her down on the bed in triumph. 'Home at last my Flora!' he cried.

She lay against the pillows and stared solemnly at him. 'I've always wondered if you'd have married me if I didn't have that Jacobite dowry,' she said.

He was astonished. 'Of course I'd marry you. I love you and I've always loved you.'

She gave a girlish little giggle. 'But we didn't know each other, did we? You were even in the redcoat army! It was One-Eyed Hugh and your father who made the match.'

'I'd have found you on my own in time. We've been meant for each other,' was his fervent reply.

Twelve

An envoy called Colonel Edmund Ryan, an officer in the French service, was enlisted by Cardinal Henry to tour the minor courts of Europe in search of a bride for his brother Charles.

Ryan had no easy task because unfortunately it turned out that no really royal or high-ranking family would consider such an alliance. Charles' bad reputation with women and alcohol was well known among the European aristocracy.

'To be sure I swear to them that he's as sober as a priest now but it makes no difference,' said Ryan when he returned from an abortive outing to tell Henry how Princess Marie Louise of Salm-Kyrburg had burst out in weeping hysterics when the proposition was put to her.

'Was she very beautiful?' asked Henry, wondering who it was that took so strongly against marrying a Stewart.

'As plain as a poor man's donkey,' said the lugubrious Ryan.

'And Princess Isabella of Mansfield only laughed when I suggested the marriage to her,' was his next piece of bad news.

Henry groaned as he saw his plans crashing around him. 'Is there anyone suitable left?' he asked.

'Only the penniless or the desperate,' was the reply.

One family fell into both categories. The next month Ryan brought news that the widowed Princess of Stolberg had four marriageable daughters and no money. Her husband Prince Gustave Adolphe of Stolberg, a minor aristocrat, had been killed at the battle of Leuthen in 1757 and left her to bring up the children alone.

As usual, the destination for dowerless girls with no rich connections was the nunnery and that was what loomed on the horizon of the Stolberg daughters when the news reached them that the Young Pretender was looking for a bride.

Already the eldest daughter Louise had, at the age of five, been made a canoness in the chapter of Saint Wandru at Mos, the same sort of aristocratic nunnery as the one at Douai that almost received Clementine so many years previously. The reclusive life did not suit her, however, and when she was sixteen she implored her mother to let her out into society in the hope of finding someone to marry her.

One likely suitor, the Marquess of Jamaica, eventually preferred her younger sister Caroline, and by the time Louise was twenty it looked as if the nunnery loomed again. Then Ryan turned up with his proposition.

The girls' mother, the Princess of Stolberg, was not going to let this fish escape and told Ryan that Charles could have his pick of either Louise or her fifteen-year-old sister. The Irishman went rushing back to Rome with this news and was met by Charles and Henry who were anxious to hear about the girls. The Irishman said the youngest girl was the prettiest of the two.

'But I think fifteen is perhaps a little too young for you. After all that makes a thirty-two-year difference in your ages,' advised Henry and Charles agreed.

'What does the twenty-year-old look like?' he asked.

'She has a good figure, a pretty enough face and excellent manners – everything your majesty can desire,' was Ryan's diplomatic reply. What he did not say was that he found Louise almost too clever and intimidatingly learned, but extremely ambitious and eager to better her circumstances.

To her even the unprepossessing, semi-literate Charles was a better prospect than the nunnery because through him she could enter society at the top level, or so she hoped.

The drawing up of the marriage contract was done by clever Henry who managed to keep it a secret because the bride's mother received a pension and many privileges from the Empress Maria Theresa who was very pro-Hanoverian in her sympathies and had no time for Jacobites.

It was essential not to annoy her till everything was finalized but when she eventually heard about the marriage she flew into a temper and banished the Princess of Stolberg from her court and withdrew her pension. It took a great deal of wheedling and self-humbling before the Princess was restored to favour.

The betrothal ceremony was conducted in secret and by proxy so the bride never met the groom while they were being pledged to each other in Paris on March 28th 1772. Ryan stood in for

Charles and looked surreptitiously from the corner of his eye at the girl by his side.

Though she was handsome enough, she had a firm, determined mouth and a calculating eye and he knew he would not want to cross her. The most striking thing about her, he thought, was the elegance and beauty of her hands which were narrow and long-fingered and which she used almost as eloquently as she used speech.

It was obvious that she was capable of turning on formidable charm if she so chose, but as a mere Irish envoy from Rome, he was not sufficiently important to attract her interest.

Ryan had little respect for Charles for he had heard the stories about his ill treatment of Clementine and his drinking bouts. *Let's hope he gets his comeuppance from this little minx*, thought the proxy bridegroom.

After the ceremony, his final task was to escort the bride to Venice by ship before riding with her to Macarata. They arrived on Good Friday, April 17th, and though that was not considered a lucky day for a wedding – especially for a Stewart for that month had been consistently unlucky for them – the bride's mother had insisted in the wedding contract that the pair be married on the first day they met in person and also that the wedding was to be consummated that same night.

Princess Stolberg was taking precautions because she had always found her sharp-tongued eldest daughter tiresome and irritating so she was allowing no opportunity for Charles to back out at the last moment, as Henry VIII had done with Anne of Cleves.

News of the proxy betrothal reached Clementine and Charlotte in Meaux even before Ryan and Louise reached Venice and they discussed it endlessly.

'I hope he behaves better with his new wife than he did with me,' said Clementine sadly.

'And I hope he doesn't forget I'm his daughter and his only descendant,' said her daughter who was now nineteen, strong-willed and very ambitious.

As she was growing up Charlotte retained and nourished her infatuation for her father who she still fondly remembered playing with her and calling her Pouponne. She regularly wrote letters to him without receiving any replies but continued to hope that hearing from her would keep his old affection warm. His lack of response did not lessen her father fixation and she told herself that if they could only meet and talk to each other again, he would love her once more.

When she heard that he was getting married, without telling her mother, she wrote him a heartfelt letter that started by congratulating him on his marriage and saying that in spite of the 'horrible void' in which he had left her, she only wished for his happiness and prosperity.

The letter was filled with the voice of an abandoned child begging for recognition. It reminded him that she had written many letters over the years without receiving any reply and she did not understand why he had abandoned her.

She pointed out that the only result she got from being his daughter was despair because she had no prospects, no means and seemed doomed to lead the 'most unhappy and most miserable life in the world.'

What she really wanted from him was not only a word of affection but his acknowledgement that she was his natural daughter.

The hardest heart would have been moved by the letter and this time it did raise a reply. Through an intermediary Charlotte was sent a message to say that Charles would accept her into his household but only if she agreed to have nothing more to do with her mother.

For Charlotte the stipulation that she had to abandon her mother was too much to ask. For years they'd had no one on earth to love except each other; they had grown together like a double-trunked tree. The love between them was unshakeable and even Charlotte's burning ambition would never allow her to agree to her father's cruel condition.

She wrote an anguished letter to him saying that she would never repudiate her mother and he replied with another ultimatum. If she wanted to retain his affection she must also agree never to marry.

She and Clementine puzzled over this and agreed that he was anxious to ensure that no child of hers could ever lay a claim to his throne.

Though he did not know it, Charles' second stipulation was

as insurmountable as his first, for Charlotte was already the mother of two small girls, Marie Victoire and Charlotte Amelie. They had been fathered by the Archbishop of Bordeaux who often came to stay at Meaux. As a cleric he was unable to marry but Charlotte and he entered into a loving relationship and she called their children her 'little flowers'.

Because the clergy protected their own, the children lived with her and her mother in the convent and no gossip escaped from its walls into the outside world.

'Is he determined to punish me? Why is he behaving like this?' she wailed as she showed her father's messages to her mother.

Clementine threw up her hands in a helpless way. 'Because he is Charles Edward Stewart. Because he is a heartbreaker.'

Thirteen

For the first few weeks of their marriage Louise de Stolberg and Charles enjoyed the only pleasant days of their time together.

When she laid eyes on the man who was to be her husband, even determined Louise quailed. He was older and more decrepit than she expected. Like many other people who only knew his story and still thought of him as the Young Chevalier, the reality of what he had become was a shock and the thought that she would have to share a bed with him was horrifying.

If her mother had not put the clause into the wedding contract about the marriage having to be consummated on the first night, it would have been Louise and not Charles who ran away.

Her disquiet softened however when she rose on her bridal morning, and found a beautiful gown of lace and gold thread waiting for her to put on. It was a gift from the Cardinal, her new brother-in-law, and after the ceremony he also presented her with another special wedding gift which weighed heavy in her hand when he handed it over. She looked at him with open delight dancing in her eyes and asked, 'It's gold, isn't it?'

He smiled, 'Yes, it is. Now look inside.'

She lifted the box's lid with careful fingers and found that under the lid there was a portrait of the Cardinal himself surrounded by diamonds and lying beneath it a banker's draft for the immense sum of 40,000 crowns – literally a king's ransom.

The Stolbergs were a poor family and during Louise's young life forty thousand crowns had not passed through the hands of them all added together.

She gasped and looked warily at the present giver, wondering what he wanted from her.

A worldly man, he could read her thoughts. 'Don't worry, my dear, I require nothing in return. It's a gift and it is entirely yours. The King of France has also agreed to pay you a pension in your own right and my brother will give you a generous allowance, I know, but this is something extra for you from me.'

She still stared in slight disbelief at this windfall wondering if Charles behaved strangely or cruelly in bed. Was she being bribed into silence? But the Cardinal had anticipated her doubts and hastened to reassure her.

'I'm not paying you to endure indignities. I only want you to keep my brother happy,' he said and although he did not add 'and sober and out of trouble', he thought it.

'I hope to do that. I've already taken my wedding vows to that effect,' she told him, knowing that in some way they would be in collusion and wondering when all would be made clear.

Henry was not a Cardinal for nothing. He had a formidable intelligence and he'd learned subtle ways during his ascent in the Vatican. Little by little, and without actually saying so, he managed to convey to Louise that he was bribing her not to become pregnant if she could possibly avoid it.

She was a clever, intuitive girl. As they came to know each other and talked, she learned to read her brother-in-law and saw in his eyes why she was being treated with such generosity.

The Cardinal was ambitious and he had achieved the highest position in the church. Short of mounting the Papal chair itself he could not go higher, but it was a different matter when he thought about who would succeed Charles as the claimant to the Stewart heritage.

To be fair to him he also wanted to end the never-ending crusade of the Stewarts to be restored to the English throne. It would never succeed, he knew, and the time had come for the whole pointless business to be ended.

Henry had always smarted because he was the second son. When Charles was young and vigorous, he accepted his position, but as his brother's health deteriorated and he failed to have an heir, Henry realized that there was a possibility of becoming king in exile himself. Even if only in name, Henry IX wanted to be the *last* Stewart king.

Marrying Charles off had been an expedient move to keep him happy and he fully expected that his brother's decrepitude might go along with an inability to reproduce, which would make the appearance of another heir unlikely.

But when he met Louise and saw how she was flourishing in youth and health, Henry had qualms. She could well have a son by Charles, or might even arrange to have herself impregnated by another man if she felt that her position would be made more secure by doing so. It was necessary for her to know there was no pressing need to conceive.

'You look as if you are a very healthy girl but if you ever need medical advice, I have access to the best doctors. Just let me know,' he said with a kindly look.

'I have no need for doctors at the moment but thank you for your consideration,' she told him and then looked across at the man she had just married. If she had any choice in the matter there would be few times when conception was likely to occur because physically Charles repulsed her and the idea of bearing his child chilled her blood.

In fact she was not a maternal woman. She had strong sexual urges and was attracted to men but her heart never warmed at the sight of babies. Growing up amongst worldly women, she knew that there were ways of avoiding conception.

The mutual tolerance of the couple's first married days did not last long and before six months had passed they were leading separate lives and stopped being even barely polite to each other.

'Where are you going?' Charles called out in a peevish voice every time he saw his wife pass by in her finery, ready to go out.

'Where are you going? I want to go with you. I want to know where you go and who you see.' His voice echoed behind her as she swept past, brushing him off like a gnat.

'I pay calls, I go to art exhibitions and in the evening I am going to the opera.' Louise stopped, turned her head and shouted back at him. He was pathologically possessive and her patience was wearing thin for he would not let her out of his sight, day or night. Fortunately he was usually too drunk at night to exercise his conjugal rights.

'But even late at night when you do come home you spend hours on your own. What are you doing then?' He sounded as peevish as a thwarted child.

'That's when I write my letters,' she told him.

He grunted in disbelief. Letter writing had never been a pastime of his and he was suspicious about who she was writing to so he repeated his threat. 'Remember if you take a lover, I'll divorce you and ruin him. Tell me where you are going!'

She laughed because in fact by that time she had not only one lover but two – young Englishmen, Danby and Coke – and biting back her irritation, she managed to become more pleasant. 'If you must know I'm going out now because a Contessa has invited me to walk in her garden.'

'But you are also always attending soirees or dinners or going to the opera. You have no time for me.'

She swung round and put on her cape as she said, 'I like Roman society. The people I meet are interesting to talk to.'

'You could talk to me.'

Her face hardened and she could not stop herself saying viciously, 'I've heard your stories about running around in the heather in Scotland so often that I can recite them by heart. I like meeting people who live real lives. They don't live in the past.'

'You should be honoured to be my wife. I am the Chevalier and you're from a very humble family. All I married you for is so that I could have a son.'

She whirled round in anger to face him. 'There's little chance of that, is there? You must be a great disappointment to the spies in your household who regularly search my laundry to see if I have stopped menstruating. Who asked them to do that? Is it your brother? If it is, tell him to stop. If I do conceive, it won't be by you, I'm afraid.'

Spies were watching her, she knew, and suspected that Henry was keeping a check to make sure she was standing by their secret bargain. If she did conceive, he would probably arrange for her to see one of the doctors he'd talked about, and so he wanted to know as early as possible.

'You'd better not take a lover or I'll divorce you,' he spat out again.

She laughed. 'No one else but you would care who fathered my child. All those people wanting a Jacobite heir would be happy to accept any son if I said it was yours. My friends sympathize with me. They know that in spite of all the women you claim to have bedded, none has given you a child. You're sterile. Perhaps you should copy your ancestor, Mary Stewart, whose son was smuggled into her bedroom in a warming pan. Do you want me to arrange a delivery like that? You're a figure of ridicule now and you'd be worse then.'

'I can make children. I have a daughter by Clementine Walkinshaw,' he protested.

'But you haven't acknowledged her as your daughter, have you? Is that because you're not sure she is really your child? Were you as impotent then as you are now?' she taunted him.

He had no answer to that but sank back in despair on his sofa with his pet dog beside him and consumed more of the wine which was too readily supplied by his Italian servants.

Finding him still languishing drunk and quarrelsome when she returned from the Contessa's garden, Louise threw up her hands in exasperation when he said, 'Will you dine with me tonight or are you going out with your friends again?'

'I told you I'm going to the opera tonight. You're fond of music, aren't you? Instead of complaining all the time, why don't you come with me?' she suggested.

He was so desperate to keep her in his sight that he agreed to the opera outing and was hauled out that evening, dressed in the height of fashion. He had to be wheeled into his opera box where he fell asleep almost instantly, only waking every now and again to be wheeled off to empty his bladder.

Louise ignored him and went off to sit with her own friends, Danby and Coke among them. A doctor in her party went to talk to Charles and came back to tell her that he thought her husband was on the verge of having an apoplectic fit.

She pretended to be shocked. 'How terrible! What can be done? Do you think he is in immediate danger?'

'The only thing that might help is if he stops drinking but I'm afraid things have gone too far and apoplexy could carry him off any minute,' the doctor said frankly. He was good at spotting potential widows who would not be grief stricken when death struck their husbands.

She clasped her lovely hands together and groaned, 'How terrible!' But inside she resolved to do nothing to curtail Charles' alcohol intake and also tried to work out how many weeks she would have to spend in mourning if he did oblige her and die soon.

The doctor was right about the apoplectic fits, which started the day after the opera outing, but though his fits were frequent, they did not kill him. In fact Charles' very strong constitution, which had seen him through the rigours of his flight in the Highlands, was saving him again. Fit followed fit, but he always recovered.

He was visibly altered by each one, however, slurring his speech and having trouble walking or using his hands. His legs became horribly ulcerated and anyone going near him had to steel themselves against the stench that came from his rotting body.

Louise and Henry kept track of his ailments with morbid fascination, both silently wondering how long he was likely to last.

But he stubbornly lived on and one day he suddenly decided that because Louise had made too many friends in Rome and she did not have enough time to devote to him, they must move to Florence.

Through agents a fine villa was rented for him from the Cesarini family and though Louise protested violently, they soon moved in.

What was worse was that immediately his health seemed to improve, and he decided that Florence suited him so well that he must buy a villa there. He had himself carried in a litter around various properties till he finally settled on a beautiful house called the Villa Guadagni which had a tower and a lovely garden.

He was so enamoured of the place that he had the Royal Stewart escutcheon and his name carved on a shield above the main staircase. When Louise saw what he was doing her heart sank because she reckoned he was intending to live there for a long time.

'How can I escape from this terrible marriage?' she asked herself over and over again, but knew that short of murdering her husband there was no way out because he seemed indestructible.

With time on her hands and without the light-hearted company of her friends and lovers in Rome, she sank into a depression which she tried to lift by going to art exhibitions. At one large show, she was touring the lines of paintings sadly pondering her situation and walking slowly along till she stopped in front of a particularly florid study of the Madonna suckling her child, when a young gallant stopped boldly beside her and asked in an Italian accent, 'Why is such a beautiful lady as you looking so sad and why are you all alone?'

She turned and stared at him, amazed at his effrontery, and saw that he was a young man of about her own age. The most unusual thing about him was his flaming red hair, the reddest she had ever seen, and he had the slim, muscular figure of a horseman.

He saw that she was standing on her dignity and gave her a brilliant smile as he said, 'Forgive me, signora, but you looked so very lonely that I thought I would cheer you by making you smile and telling you that you have the most beautiful hands I have ever seen. I'm a poet and I could write an ode to them.'

Louise spread out her hands and stared down at them. They were one of her best features, she knew. When she did that, he saw how magnificent her jewellery was, for the rings she was wearing over her thin silk gloves were set with stones that had to be worth a fortune.

He'd thought she was just a bored upper-class wife passing the time in the art gallery, but now he realized that she obviously was someone very special and very rich. He made a deep bow and swept off his cockaded hat.

'Vittorio Alfieri, signora,' he said by way of introduction.

Normally she would have severely corrected anyone who did not use her title but it was obvious that this young man had no idea who she was. Pleased by his compliments, she smiled at him, noticing that he had a strong, intelligent face. A spark of sexual attraction sprang from him to her and back again. It fluttered in her stomach like a trapped bird and surprised her because she had never felt like that before.

'You say you're a poet? Do I know any of your works?' she asked flirtatiously.

He beamed. 'You might have seen my recent play, *Cleopatra*, or my *Filippo*?'

She was delighted. 'Indeed I have seen them both. They are such moving tragedies that they almost broke my heart. You must be the famous Count Alfieri.'

'And you are obviously a woman of culture.'

'And a Princess. I am the wife of the Duke of Albany.'

He stepped back and his face showed concern for her. 'You mean the Stewart pretender? I apologize if I am being too outspoken but how can a beautiful woman like you be married to such a miserable man? It's like seeing a flower in the fingers of a clown.'

She was obviously not offended for she laughed and said, 'So you know my husband then? But royal marriages are not made for love, Count Alfieri. Your tragedies must have taught you that.'

'Then you need a *cavaliere servante*,' he said, taking her hand again.

'Do you think you could fill that position for me?' she flirted, remembering rumours she had heard about the many romances that Alfieri was said to have conducted.

Wasn't there something about him fighting a duel with a lord in London's Hyde Park, over the lord's wife? The spirit of rebellion in Louise's nature thrilled to that.

What was to be a lifelong passion for both of them began that day as they stood surrounded by landscapes and paintings of religious themes that neither of them looked at because they only had eyes for each other.

For the first time in her life Louise was in love.

That afternoon Alfieri was invited to the Palazzo Guadagni and ingratiated himself with Charles by admiring its magnificence and, over the weeks that followed, while he started making love to Louise, he won Charles' confidence by writing a play about Mary Queen of Scots, which was very admiring of the Stewart dynasty.

Alfieri was also good at enduring the telling and re-telling of the stories about the long-past adventures in the Scottish Highlands. He sat by the cuckolded husband's side nodding his head and wondering how the wreck of a man before him had managed to endure such sufferings, and rightly guessed that Charles' derring-do was bolstered by strong drink and the bravery of other people.

It was difficult for him and Louise to find places and ways of making love, for Charles was always watchful and so were his servants, but they did succeed from time to time and if they did not, abstinence only fuelled their passion.

When they were apart Alfieri found consolation in writing her love poems which bemoaned the fact that she was sharing a bed, not with him, but with the physical, stinking wreck that was her husband.

When they were together, it was difficult for them to keep their hands off each other and one day, thinking that Charles was asleep on the sofa beside them, they allowed themselves to embrace and were locked in a passionate clinch when he woke up and realized what was going on.

Servants were summoned and Alfieri was thrown out of the house while Charles took his fury out on his wife, seizing her by the throat and nearly throttling her. Then he threw her on to the bed and tried, not very successfully, to rape her.

Louise was no Clementine. She was not going to stay with him and endure ill treatment like that. She determined that plans had to be made so she could escape from the Palazzo Guadagni as soon as possible. As far as cunning and intelligence was concerned, she was infinitely more capable than her husband and she laid her plans well.

On the face of it, she forgave Charles for his outburst and Alfieri did not reappear in their villa. However, she found an eager accomplice in a female friend called Madame Olivia Orlandini, an Irish woman, who clucked in horror when told how Charles had almost strangled his wife. 'The brute!' she cried.

Louise sobbed when she showed her bruises and told her story. 'I have to get away from him or he will certainly kill me. That's why his mistress, the Scottish woman who had his daughter, left him too. She was afraid for her life and she had to take refuge in a convent.'

Olivia loved a good drama and this one was very much to her taste. 'We'll make plans. I'll help you get away from him,' she promised.

'But he watches me round the clock, and so do his servants. He sends three of them with me if I even go into the garden,' moaned Louise.

'I'm sure we can work something out,' Olivia told her so they put their heads together and started plotting.

One morning a few days later Louise told Charles that her friend Madame Orlandini was coming to breakfast and they intended to go together to a certain convent that was renowned for the fine needlework of its nuns.

As usual Charles was suspicious of her going out without him, and insisted on accompanying them, but that was what she had expected to happen.

'But you have no interest in needlework,' she pretended to protest weakly.

'I have an interest in keeping my eye on you,' was his reply and when Olivia arrived they both had to keep their patience and endure the protracted waiting while he was dressed and conveyed to his carriage.

The nunnery was not far away and as they neared it, Madame Orlandini glanced out of the window and exclaimed, 'Why, there's a friend of mine. Let's take him with us!'

The carriage was stopped and a young Irishman called Geoghegan climbed in. Charles was none too pleased because by this time he was suspicious of any younger, fitter men who came near his wife, but Geoghegan, with fluent Irish charm, went out of his way to flatter the old man. At the nunnery he offered to help the decrepit Prince to mount the flight of stairs to the main door while the women ran on ahead.

In fact the nunnery had been specially chosen because of its steep steps and Geoghegan was more of a hindrance than a help. By the time Charles reached the top step, clinging limpet-like to the Irishman's arm, the door was firmly shut against them.

'Knock on it!' he ordered and Geoghegan did as he was told but there was no response.

'Knock again,' said Charles.

There was still no response. Only on the third knocking a small grille in the door opened and a stern-looking eye stared back at them.

'What do you want?' a hidden nun asked.

'I am the Duke of Albany and my wife has just entered your nunnery. I want to join her,' Charles said proudly.

'I am the Mother Superior of this order and you can't come in. Your wife has taken refuge with us. Go away!' was the abrupt reply and the grille was slammed shut.

He could not believe it. Once again the church had foiled his attempt to recover his woman. He was incandescent with rage because he thought he heard Louise laughing behind the huge wooden door and he threatened to run Geoghegan through with his sword, except that he was not wearing one and so the young Irishman laughed too at the empty threat.

Letters were soon on their way from Florence to Cardinal Henry in Rome who read them with much satisfaction. If Louise had run away there was no chance of her bearing another heir to the Stewart line.

Fourteen

Olivia and Louise were jubilant that they had pulled off the escape with so little trouble.

'You're a clever woman. You'll outfox that man you're married to because he's a brainless fool,' Olivia told her friend.

'Being brainless seems to keep him alive. When is he going to die? He should have gone years ago. When I married him I thought I'd be widowed within a couple of years but it's been nearly five. God knows, he drinks enough to float a fleet and the doctors have all given up on him but he keeps on going!'

'It's a good idea to go back to Rome. You have a good rapport with your brother-in-law the Cardinal, and if you appear devout and stay in a convent he'll support you against his brother, won't he?' said Olivia.

'I've written him a letter telling the reasons I left my husband. I said that if I stayed with him he might kill me. Cardinal Henry is anxious to stop Charles doing anything worse than he's done already. The woman who bore his daughter got the same brutal treatment but she kept it secret but I'm not prepared to shut my mouth and the Cardinal knows that what I say is true.'

A week later Louise was on her way out of Florence riding in a fine carriage with an escort of armed men provided by the Cardinal. Henry had arranged accommodation for her in the Ursuline Convent of Trastavere at Rome. When Charles found out where she was, insult was added to injury because the Roman nuns took care to spread the news that his runaway wife was lodged in the room once occupied by his mother Clementina when she ran away from his father almost fifty years before.

As she took leave of her friend Olivia, Louise said, 'I won't be staying in a convent there any longer than I have to because I married my pig of a husband to get out of one and I'm determined not to end up there again. I'm asking for a separation and moving to Rome will make it easier to go back into society. My husband is liable to turn up anywhere here in Florence.'

Olivia nodded in fervent agreement. Convent life did not attract her either. 'But what about your *cavaliere servante*, Vittorio? Does the Cardinal know about him?' she wanted to know.

Louise glared at her friend. 'Of course not. He's a churchman, isn't he? I'm not eager for him to find out that I have a lover and so it must be kept secret.'

Olivia loved a conspiracy. 'My lips are sealed and I'll do anything I can to help you,' she promised.

'I have to see him. I have to kiss him,' Louise sobbed.

A thrilled Olivia patted her back as she said, 'You will, my dear, you will. I'll help you. Love like yours can't be denied.'

Reverting to practicality, Louise went on, 'I want you to arrange for our correspondence, Olivia. Vittorio and I write to each other every day and I want him to send his letters to you and you can send them on to me. He writes the most wonderful poems telling me how much he loves me and wants to see me. We're both burning up with love and having to hide away is killing me. I dream about him every night and I know he dreams about me. I wake in a terrible sweat of longing for him.'

She was a very physical woman and lack of love was making her distraught. Snatched love making with Alfieri had dominated her life for the past year and celibacy did not suit her. Nor did it suit him. Their letters were so passionate that the words almost burned off the page.

She was right about Henry being prepared to help her. He was genuinely afraid that Charles would commit some terrible act if he got his hands on his runaway wife because he also bombarded his brother with letters accusing her of adultery, an accusation that Henry disbelieved because he was beguiled by the seeming sincerity of the letters he received from Louise.

After consultations with his brother's doctors, he shared Louise's opinion that Charles must die soon, and hoped that when it happened, he, Henry, would still be fit and well enough to become a king in exile.

When she began to show signs of fretfulness about being shut up in another convent, he sent her a letter inviting her to take up residence in the Palazzo Cancellaria, the magnificent Cardinalate palace in Rome that he used only rarely because he spent most of his time in Frascati where the climate was less oppressive and suited him better.

She gave a gasp of delight when she read this message. To live in great style in Henry's luxurious palace suited her very well. She had many friends in the city and knew that it would be easy to resume her affair with Alfieri under cover of social events.

'Thank you, thank you, dear brother-in-law,' she wrote back to Henry.

On the first night she was installed in the Cardinal's Palazzo, Alfieri was able to slip into her bed and they made vigorous love till dawn.

When he left he stood staring up at the morning sky that was streaked with all the colours of the rainbow. With a wild whoop, he threw his hat in the air, leaped on to his horse and galloped off like a madman.

He knew that now his love was with him again, he would be able to write his best work ever and plunged into an orgy of production that made him the most prominent literary figure in Italy.

They were often seen out together but were always very discreet in the way they behaved in public. Though shrewd, Henry never guessed how deeply they were involved with each other because they acted the part of only being casual acquaintances superbly.

When he was not writing his plays and, more secretly, penning love poems for Louise, Alfieri spent a great deal of time with his horses because he was a renowned horseman with a large stable of magnificent animals.

He even pretended to be enamoured of various other women, and though she knew that he was only putting up a front, these flirtations always aroused furious jealousy in Louise.

'I am your muse and your only muse. I wish I could proclaim that to the whole world,' she cried when they made up after one fight.

'You know you have my heart,' he told her and stifled her protests with kisses.

In spite of a niggling anxiety that her husband might turn up in Rome and make trouble for her, Louise was deliriously happy. She went out in society as the Countess of Albany, and provided herself with a retinue of servants dressed in magnificent red and gold livery.

Every big social occasion was honoured by her presence and people bowed before her as if she was genuine royalty. They were not all as gullible as Henry about the relationship between her and Alfieri but he was the literary star of society, and as his mistress she was able to gather a group of intellectuals into her orbit. Her salons in the Cardinal's palace became the most coveted social venues in the city. Anyone with pretensions of any sort, social or intellectual, fought for an invitation.

Back in Florence Charles raged impotently because spies and troublemakers regularly brought him news of his runaway wife – and her secret lover.

Also left behind in Florence, Olivia, Louise's Irish confidante, could not keep a curb on her tongue and was unable to resist boasting to her friends about how involved she was in the romance between Louise and Alfieri. What she said inevitably made its way back to Charles.

'My wife thinks herself very clever but she should have known better than entrust her secrets to a chatterbox Irish woman,' he said bitterly.

Letters with damning circumstantial details were fired off by him to Henry until even he was forced to start doubting Louise. What disillusioned him in the end was that the lovers grew more careless as time went on and even the Cardinal was surprised by their flagrant shows in public of more than mild affection.

It did not really matter to him if Louise took lovers but she had to be discreet and he feared that she was in danger of forgetting decorum. After all, Henry told himself, he himself lived a sexual life of secrets, but he could not be seen to be allowing his brother to be openly cuckolded in his own palace!

Magnificent in his flowing robes, he arrived at his Palace one winter day only to be told that the Countess of Albany was out riding with Count Alfieri, so he sat down to wait for her with his hands folded in his lap and his face impassive.

When they arrived back, a servant halted her at the door to tell her that the Cardinal had arrived and wished to see her. Sending Alfieri away, she ran up the stairs and burst into the drawing room, smiling and exclaiming in delight at this unexpected visit.

She was always effusive towards Henry but in truth she was much more scared of him than she was of his brother. Polished and hardened by his ascent through the ranks of the Vatican clergy, Henry was impossible to read. A master of diplomacy, he was always exquisitely polite but no one could ever be sure what he was thinking.

He did not stand up when she knelt beside him, but held out his hand for her to kiss. 'It is a pleasure to see you, dear sister-in-law. I hope you are comfortable here in my palace,' he said.

She did not miss the implication but calmly took a chair and hurried to reassure him, 'I am very comfortable and very grateful that you have rescued me from that brute.'

Henry nodded. 'My brother writes to me that he has heard some scurrilous rumours about the way you are living here in Rome. He says you have a paramour.'

She managed to look outraged. 'He is only trying to blacken my name,' she protested but she did not ask the identity of the paramour and Henry did not tell her.

'My brother is a vengeful man so it is necessary that you ensure he has no grounds for spreading these stories about you, my dear.' His tone was conciliatory and she knew what she was being told.

She nodded silently and listened as Henry went on, 'If there was any man whose name is linked with yours, even if you are innocent, I suggest he leaves Rome at once. Perhaps he might like to go to Naples?'

Louise's high spirits dropped at once. She had never been to Naples, which was at least two days' journey away, but she knew that was where Alfieri must go if she was to keep her position in Rome, her place in the Cardinal's palace and, in fact, her physical safety. At a whim Henry could send her back to her husband and what would happen to her then?

'I will make sure that my conduct does not give rise to any suggestion that my husband is being wronged by me,' she said solemnly.

Henry smiled and she noticed that his eyes were as black and as blank as obsidian. She knew she would have to be very careful.

For a year she and Alfieri were thrown back into painful separation, writing yearning letters to each other and bemoaning the fact that Charles still stubbornly refused to die and make Louise a widow.

For his part he was mouldering away in his Florentine palace, his health degenerating with every day that passed. People who went to visit him never stayed long in his room and the more sensitive among them often came out retching because he smelled so foul. He gave off a stink of corrupting flesh.

In 1784, hearing about the sad state of a fellow monarch, even a pretending one, kindly King Gustavus III of Sweden, who was on a tour of Italy, called on Charles and was horrified by the state in which he found him.

Charles, wig awry and with pus-soaked bandages adorning his legs, was lying on a sofa with his pet dog on his lap and a bottle of brandy close at hand.

'My dear man, you must pull yourself together,' exclaimed Gustavus.

'Why should I? My wife has taken off with a red-haired scribbler of verse and left me here, hoping that I'll die,' was the self-pitying reply.

'Someone should help you regularize your affairs and way of life. What does your brother think?' said Gustavus who had a Nordic horror of dirt and disorder.

'My brother is as bad as my wife. He can hardly wait for me to die so he can sign himself as king in my place. He's taken in my wife and is allowing her to carry on her affair in his palace in Rome while she lives off my money.'

'Tut tut, that's not good. I think it would be best for all of you if you could arrange a divorce.'

Charles looked at his visitor with scorn. 'A divorce? It would almost be easier to be reborn than for me to get a divorce in the Vatican.'

Gustavus knew that was true. 'A legal separation then?' he suggested.

Charles looked interested. In truth he did not miss Louise but he hated being cuckolded and gossiped about. He wanted to be the injured party who took steps to get rid of the guilty one. Besides, Louise was still spending his money and flaunting herself around in jewels that belonged to his family, particularly to the Sobieskis, and he wanted them back.

'Do you think that would be possible?' he asked.

Gustavus replied, 'To a king, anything is possible.'

But not a divorce, thought Charles.

Strings were pulled; money was spent and in the summer of 1784 a deed of separation was drawn up between Charles and Louise.

She read the document carefully and made no protests about the stipulations. 'It doesn't matter to me that I can't use his name any longer. He calls himself Charles III but it's an empty claim,' she told her lawyer.

'How do you want to be referred to in future then?' he asked.

'Duchess of Albany,' she said.

'He's also refusing to pay your allowance,' the lawyer pointed out.

'I don't care about that either. He can keep his money. I have a pension from Marie Antoinette and he can't touch that.'

'He wants the Sobieski jewels.'

'He can have them but if I send back the jewels I want him to send me all the clothes I left in Florence.' Louise was very stylish and had a magnificent wardrobe which she had been forced to leave behind when she fled.

'I'll write to him to that effect,' said the lawyer, who admired her sangfroid as she stripped a pair of magnificent rings off her finger and went to put them in a jewel casket that contained even more valuable pieces, which she handed to him.

Henry too was astonished at her eagerness to be obliging.

'You are being very generous,' he said and she turned to him with a smile.

'It's worth doing without fripperies if I can be rid of him forever.'

It was a good thing that she was indifferent to possessions because Charles never sent back her clothes.

She was so eager to sign the separation papers because she thought that living a separate life from her husband would mean that Alfieri and she could be together at last. Money did not matter too much because Alfieri was very rich from the profits of his many plays. In fact he was probably richer than Charles, but unlikely to hold on to it for long because he was also prodigal with money.

At least he was able to accumulate funds without begging for them, she thought, because she knew that Charles still spent much time writing to the crowned heads of Europe pleading poverty while all the time living like the king he thought he was.

His last appeal to the King of Spain yielded him a pension of 1000 piastres a year, hardly enough to maintain his army of Italian servants. All the loyal Scottish Jacobite hangers-on who used to work for nothing for his father had long ago disappeared.

When she wrote to tell Alfieri that her separation was about to be finalized, he wrote to tell her that he was heading for Siena with forty fine horses he had bought, one for each of the plays he had written. He would meet her anywhere as soon as she was free.

As soon as all the signatures on the deed of separation were in place, Louise could contain herself no longer and sent a message to tell him to go to Colmar on the Rhine where one of her friends owned a castle.

'It is best we don't meet openly in Italy yet. I am still afraid that the Cardinal might make trouble for me if he thinks I have a lover so soon,' she wrote. But Alfieri was already on the road to meet her and she knew his cavalcade of horses would attract immense attention as he rode along. She was proud at the thought of the magnificent impression he must be making.

'I am quite worn out after all the negotiations with my husband and I've been advised to take the waters at Baden,' she told Henry. He was still regarding her with suspicion, wondering what her easy acquiescence about the terms of the separation meant. Did she have another man waiting in the wings?

'That's a very good idea, my dear. Go to Baden and recover your health,' he told her smoothly.

She did not need any more encouragement but took to the road at once with a cavalcade of protective servants. They wasted no time and at eight o'clock in the morning three days later she jumped off her horse in the courtyard of an inn at Colmar where she knew Alfieri had taken up residence.

He was eating breakfast when he heard the clattering of hooves in the yard and ran out to catch her in his arms and cover her face with kisses, no longer caring if other people could see these manifestations of their love.

In tears she kissed him back and clung to him with both hands. 'At last, at last,' they chorused together and ran to his room in the inn. Her friend's castle was forgotten. They preferred to make love in the room at the inn where they stayed without emerging for three days.

Life in the Villa Guadagni after Louise left was boring. Charles had no one to bully, no one to taunt and he could not understand why Florentine society shunned him now that his wife had gone away.

He passed his time trying to engage any passing servant in conversation and, over and over again, telling his doctors and anyone else who would listen about his bravery during 1746 when he was on the run in the Highlands.

He was very aware that he needed a new audience; he needed someone who was too intimidated by him not to walk away. Another wife seemed out of the question. Women were more trouble than they were worth. Besides, since he was only separated and not divorced, he was not in a position to marry.

When he was at his lowest ebb, he remembered that he had a daughter, a girl who, judging by her letters, would do whatever he asked.

Lying in his bed with his pet dog tucked in by his side, he dictated a letter to his secretary.

Fifteen

'It is a miracle!' Clementine clasped her hands in delight after she read the letter which had arrived for her daughter that morning.

'He's acknowledged me at last. He says here that I am his daughter,' said Charlotte, leaning over her mother's shoulder and pointing out the words on the paper to her.

Clementine asked to re-read the letter herself. Over the years she'd learned to suspect everything Charles did or said. But there it was in writing and there was no mistaking it. He acknowledged Charlotte as his child and invited her to go to Florence to join him.

She felt dazed as she looked up at her daughter. It had taken thirty-one years but he'd done the decent thing at last by acknowledging fatherhood of their child who so badly wanted to be acknowledged.

She looked at her daughter through a film of tears and thought that she was physically very like her father as he had been when she first saw him. Charlotte was tall for a woman, erect and well built, light-haired and with the same aristocratic profile and fair-skinned face as her father. Fortunately she was not given to his capriciousness or mood swings but was kind-hearted, with humour and gaiety as well as a large share of his charm, which, Clementine knew only too well, could be beguiling to those on whom he turned it. *Thank God*, she thought, *my child is a kind and feeling person who does not have his utter selfishness.*

'You have waited a long time for this, my darling,' she said.

Charlotte was beaming in delight. 'I always believed he would acknowledge me at last. I remember how he used to love me. He played with me and called me Pouponne. He really loved me then and I loved him so I knew that the power of love would bring us back together.'

Clementine sighed. Love, she thought, had been her own downfall. It was a great deceiver. She'd loved Charles once, and in fact loved him still in spite of everything that had happened, but she doubted now if he had ever really loved anyone except himself. *Don't let love lead my girl into similar disillusion*, she silently prayed.

'But I wonder why he has done this now?' she said in a worried voice.

The scandal of Charles' marital confusions had reached their secluded French convent and the last news she had of him was that his wife had left him for an Italian playwright and they were legally separated.

'Perhaps he's lonely now that his wife has gone. And he has no official heir. He'll be worried about what will happen to the Stewart claim when he dies,' she suggested but secretly hoped that he had remembered all the letters their daughter wrote to him and was overcome with longing to see his long-lost child.

'I'm sure he's missed me all those years and wants to see me at last. Oh, I wish I could go to him today. This could be the turn of all our fortunes, yours and my children's as well,' Charlotte cried.

Clementine felt pity for her yearning daughter and said, 'I'm sure you're right but he's very changeable. You'll have to take care because he won't take kindly to you having children. Remember when he wrote and said you must never marry. What you have to do now is write and say you are eager to join him in Florence and wait for him to make the travel arrangements. If he really wants to see you he'll certainly send an escort to take you to Italy,' she said, remembering her own long wait in Scotland before her laggard lover sent for her and her disappointing arrival at Douai.

It was a fight to hide her misgivings when she had another flashback to the times when Charles attacked her with murderous rage, but, she thought, surely time had mellowed him and anyway he had never been violent towards their daughter, only to her.

Charlotte should be quite safe. She also feared that if her daughter did not go to Florence she would miss any chance of being reunited with her father and finding her true place in society.

What would be the reaction of Charles and his Cardinal brother Henry if Charlotte's clandestine domestic life and trio of illegitimate children were revealed, for by now the archbishop had fathered three children on Charles' daughter as Charlotte's two little girls had recently been joined by a three-month-old baby boy who Charlotte christened Charles Edward after the grandfather who neither knew nor cared about his existence.

If Henry found that out, he might withdraw the pension he still sent to them every year and which, as Clementine's main means of support, had sustained them ever since she ran away from Charles.

She kept in regular touch with Henry, of whom she was greatly in awe, and wrote frequently to him thanking him for his consideration and kindness. When he asked her to confirm Charlotte's bastardy, she had been willing to do whatever he wanted but if Charles now decided to acknowledge his daughter, how would Henry react?

Would he fear being displaced as next in line for the Stewart kingdom? She feared that her daughter was about to start a dangerous journey with traps set to catch her all along the way. It was all very worrying, with motives and sub-motives that were totally unpredictable.

Clementine looked round their little chamber. It was not large but it was comfortable and homely, and suddenly she wished that the letter from Florence had never arrived. She could not attempt to persuade her daughter to give up her dream of seeing her father again but experience had taught her to have very disquieting fears about anything in which Charles was involved and she was very reluctant to lose her daughter for they had an unbreakable bond.

Since her birth Charlotte had been Clementine's reason for living and the love between them was uncritical and solid. She had no wish to see her tight little family of grandmother, mother, and grandchildren broken up. They all lived in happy seclusion in their French convent – or had until now – but a chill of fear seized her when she saw how enthusiastic Charlotte was about leaving.

Clementine laid the back of her hand on her forehead and gave a low sigh, wishing she had never had anything to do with Charles. She remembered the raging anger of her sister Catherine in St James' Palace and thought that perhaps Catherine had been right from the beginning. Would it have been better to have stayed at home and forgotten all about him?

But when she looked across at her daughter, her heart filled with love for she knew that if she'd stayed, she would never have given birth to this dear child. The only good thing that came out of her passion was her precious girl.

Charlotte saw her mother's disquiet and took her hand. 'What's wrong? Do you think I should refuse to go to meet him?' she asked, looking down again at the letter. She had longed for it so and now that it had come, she was suddenly afraid.

'Of course you must go, but I'm afraid that you will stay away too long and forget us,' her mother said.

'I promise, of course I promise to come back soon. I love you all too much to stay away for long. I'm sure I'll be able to talk to my father and he'll understand about my family. He might even allow us all to live together in Florence, and I'll make sure he provides more money for you as well. This is the turn of our fortunes, Mama!' cried Charlotte fervently.

Once more Charles threw out offers but did nothing to expedite them and for the next six months, every time a letter arrived they looked at it with apprehension before breaking the seal, but it was never from Charles.

Charlotte had almost given up her dream of seeing him again when the summons did arrive and it was carried by an official escort who was to accompany her on her journey.

'But I need a few days to prepare,' she protested.

Once again Ryan had been put in charge of escort duty and he was not inclined to linger. 'My master is anxious that you come at once,' he told the young woman.

'But these things take time.' She was anguished in case he found out about her secret children. Eventually he agreed to go away and return for her in three days, by which time she would be ready to leave. Then she ran to her mother's rooms to break the news.

'I'm summoned to Florence,' she said in a quavering voice, and then burst into tears.

'Do you still want to go?' asked her mother, looking up from her sewing.

The answer was vehement. 'Oh yes, I long to see him again. His messenger says that he needs me so I must go.'

'Did he really say he needs you?'

'Yes, exactly that.'

Clementine shook her head, remembering the letter she herself received from Charles telling her that he needed her. How many tears had that letter cost her?

Charlotte knelt by her chair and took her hand. 'As soon as I can I'll send for you and my babies. This can only be good for us all. It will secure our financial future, I'll make sure of that.'

Clementine knew what an opportunity this was for her daughter. 'Oh, my dear, you must write to me and tell me everything that happens. I'll look after the babies. But what are you going to tell Rohan?'

'He knows now I want to be reconciled with my father and he accepts that our association must be kept secret. What a scandal it would be for him if our secret got out. We've broken all sorts of rules.'

'But he loves you. He's been a good man to us all and he loves his children though he can't acknowledge them.' Rohan was not as free as Charles, who could have acknowledged his daughter from the beginning but chose not to do so until he found himself alone and unloved, Clementine thought.

Charlotte was well aware of the complications of her situation. 'I won't be able to write directly to Rohan because there are probably spies in my father's house and everything I write might be read so my letters will be sent to you and you must share them with him. And also let me know how he does. I'll be jealous in case he finds another woman because I do love him, you know.'

Many tears were shed over the next two days and Charlotte found herself alternating between grief and high excitement while her mother and the babies clung to her in tears. 'I will do my best to send for you,' she promised. 'It might take time but I'm sure I'll win my father round.'

She arranged a meeting with her lover Rohan, who shared Clementine's apprehensions about her travelling to join the Young Pretender's Florentine court but could say nothing to dissuade her. Because he was a churchman he could not accept paternity of his children so Clementine was made their official guardian.

'I will write to you every day and I want you to write back but you must not mention the children by name. We will call them *mes fleurs*,' she told her mother.

When she bid farewell to her lover he asked, 'Will this be forever?'

She took his hands as she said, 'Of course not. It will only be till I feel secure enough with my father to tell him about the children.'

When she and Ryan clattered out through the convent gate on fine chestnut horses, her mother sat at an upper window with the children beside her and they were all weeping.

Meeting her father again was a shock to Charlotte. The man she remembered as bright-eyed, laughing and playful had become a physical wreck, lying with his snarling lap dog on a soiled sofa with smirking servants giving him drinks whenever he lifted a languid hand. The smell that came from him filled the room but she hid her nausea and ran over to kneel at the side of his sofa and kiss his cheek.

'Oh, Papa, how wonderful to see you again after so many years!' she cried.

Charles beamed at her. There was nothing he enjoyed so much as devotion and flattery. Obviously he'd done the right thing by bringing this young woman from France to take care of him, he thought. She was his daughter and therefore not so likely to make unreasonable claims on him like Louise, that harridan of a wife he'd got rid of. By this time he had convinced himself that he'd sent her away and she had not gone of her own accord.

His rheumy eyes surveyed his long-lost daughter. Pouponne had grown into a rangy-looking woman and the idea occurred to him that perhaps he'd looked a little like her when he'd dressed as Betty Burke, because she was tall and fairly heavily built, not as feminine as her mother, though as far as he could remember Clementine had never struck him as beautiful. Beauty in women was lost on him anyway. It usually brought trouble with it.

'My daughter!' he said theatrically, thinking how much this new arrival was going to annoy his brother because Henry had made no secret of his disapproval when he had decided to declare Charlotte legitimate. How much more angry would he be if she was to be set up as his heir and potentially the next Stewart claimant. He had not gone that far yet but if she suited him, he might do it soon.

'You won't leave me?' he asked in a quavering voice, suddenly becoming pathetic.

She was visibly moved. Tears sparkled in her eyes and she knelt by his side as she answered, 'As long as you want me, I promise I won't leave you.'

The love that she had nursed for him over the years was in full flower and she was prepared to dedicate herself to him. To do her justice her devotion was not only for selfish reasons though she hoped to be able to make her mother's life more comfortable and ensure a good future for her '*fleurs*', but she also longed to help him, keep him company in his old age and make him happy.

She failed to realize that the man who lay on the sofa beside her was not only an ailing old man, eking out his last years in loneliness and misery, but a selfish exploiter. To her he was her father and she would do everything she could to make the last years of his life comfortable because on their journey Ryan had told her that Charles was grievously ill and not expected to live very long.

'He has a life expectancy of less than a year according to the doctors,' he'd said lugubriously.

They did not reckon on Charles' marvellous powers of recuperation, however. Delighted by his daughter's obvious devotion, he set about launching her into society and embarked on a busy new social round. Carried in a litter with damask and velvet curtains, he took her to the opera and threw lavish receptions, taking much pleasure in seeing the curiosity she aroused in Florentine society for everyone who was anyone rushed to see her.

Though she was no beauty, she had polished manners and was intelligent, so she made a good impression and he insisted that when they went out or entertained, she appeared in the magnificent Sobieski jewels.

Seeing how they sparkled round her neck and on her arms and fingers, he took much pleasure in knowing that Louise had been forced to relinquish them. He was never going to let them out of his sight again and was certainly not yet prepared to give them to his daughter though he liked to see her wearing them.

She handled the huge emeralds and rubies in awe for they

were so large they seemed unreal. One alone, she guessed, would keep her mother in comfort for the rest of her life, but she knew better than ask her father to give her anything because she soon recognized that in his old age, like his father, he had become compulsively protective of his money and treasures.

Much of his conversation, when not recounting his adventures in Scotland, was about how poor he was and she had to write letters for him to various people pleading for money. Yet even as she wrote, she knew that the price of one Sobieski necklace would keep all the poorer inhabitants of the cities of Florence or Rome in food for a year.

Lulled into good temper by her attentive attendance on him, Charles insisted on throwing weekly balls in his Palazzo though he could not himself dance any longer and slept through most of the proceedings.

He also attended every opera that was staged and had his box redecorated with yellow silk curtains and deeply fringed golden pelmets. He slept through the operas as well.

He announced that his daughter was to be addressed as the Duchess of Albany and must be treated like royalty. In a very grandiose ceremony he invested her with the ancient Scottish Order of the Thistle, which she was required to wear on her breast on every social occasion.

He also commissioned medals to be struck in her honour. They bore her profile and a Latin motto that translated as 'There is one hope.' This was a direct jab at Henry because he took a cruel delight in guessing how much his aggrandization of Charlotte was antagonizing his brother.

The Cardinal only shook his head when people brought him news of his brother's apparent renewal of life after the arrival of Charlotte. He knew better than to rise in rage or show jealousy at Charles' attempts to annoy him, because he knew very well what his brother was doing. Charles wanted Henry to be annoyed but he could throw as many balls and load her with as many decorations as he liked as far as Henry was concerned. At least they were well out of his way in Florence.

Once his daughter was successfully launched in society, with people flocking to see her and exclaiming over her natural charm and eagerness to please, Charles began to feel that he had exhausted the potential of Florence and decided, with the same rapidity and lack of consultation as he always made decisions, that they should move to Henry's home ground, Rome, and take on society there as well.

'We're going to Rome. You'll like it there because it's far less provincial than this place,' he told Charlotte.

She looked surprised. Life in Florence suited her very well. If he thought it was provincial, she secretly wondered what he would have made of the lives she and her mother lived in rural France.

'When do we go?' she asked apprehensively. She had been with him for almost a year and was fretting for her loved ones because she had thought he would be dead by now.

'Tomorrow. Get your servants to pack your trunks.'

'Where will we live in Rome?'

'In my father's old Palazzo Muti. I've sent orders to my brother telling him to make sure that it's cleaned for our arrival and when we get there, I'll have it properly decorated for us. I did it up a little when I was married to Louise but the place was falling apart when my father lived there. He hated spending money,' said Charles.

Over the years messengers going to and fro between her mother and her grandfather and uncle had provided Charlotte with a fair idea of what to expect at the Palazzo Muti. Grandly, Charles put her in charge of the project, saying, 'It will give you something positive to do.' She welcomed the project because it would give her a break from the hours she spent listening to her father going over and over the same stories about his past adventures.

It was difficult to keep an expression of rapt attention on her face when he launched himself into the same story for the third time in an hour, for his mind was beginning to ramble, but he was her father and could not live much longer. She had taken on the responsibility of easing his old age and it was obvious that listening was very much part of that.

On the eve of their leaving Florence, he told her, 'You must come and help when my serving men carry out my boxes before we go,' he said.

'Can't the men do that themselves?' she asked.

'They can pack my clothes and books but there are some

things that I don't entrust entirely to them without supervision and I want you there to make sure there is no thieving. We'll do it tomorrow.'

He had a crafty look in his eye and she wondered what he was hiding for he had already shown her the Sobieski jewel box from which he pulled out necklaces and bracelets for her to wear when she went to the opera with him. He always insisted on watching them being put back again when the evening was over, and she wondered if he suspected that she might keep something back for herself.

'I'll help you,' she promised and went to her own chamber to write an urgent letter to her mother giving news of the move to Rome. She and Clementine exchanged a steady stream of letters – as many as three or four each a week – and when one addressed in her mother's hand arrived for Charlotte her heart always ached because the sight of it transported her back to the convent.

She missed Meaux badly; she missed her dear children and she missed her lover, but it was impossible for her to receive any detailed news of them because she was afraid that if the children's existence was revealed, Charles would throw her out. After all, she'd already spent a year tending for him and did not want to waste her efforts now.

Surely this exile will not last long, she told herself, because her father was obviously still very ill and his outings to balls and operas were usually followed by an apoplectic fit. Over and over again his doctors shook their heads and warned her that the next big attack would probably kill him, but he went on living.

When his chief doctor heard that he was planning to travel to Rome, he told Charlotte to prepare herself for Charles' death. The rigours of the journey, even though his patient would travel in a litter slung between horses, might well prove fatal, he said.

Next morning, while the house throbbed with the thud of running feet and the bumping of trunks and boxes, she went to her father's bedchamber and found him sitting up in bed looking very spry, as if the prospect of the journey was actually enlivening him.

'Send the servants away,' he told her and when the door closed behind his valet, he sat forward and said, 'Look under my bed. There's a box bound with brass there. Can you haul it out?'

She knelt down and saw the box which was large and very solid looking. She tried but could not move it because she was not strong and had recently started suffering from debilitating stomach upsets that left her weak and nauseous. She wanted to please him however and grasped one of the handles set in the side of the box and gave it a firm pull but only succeeded in moving it a couple of inches.

He was leaning over the edge of the bed watching and she told him, 'I'm not strong enough to move it.'

He made an exasperated noise and said, 'You look strong enough to me but if you can't shift it, we'll be forced to get that valet of mine in. Call him for me.'

When she ran across and opened the door, the valet almost fell in on top of her. It was obvious that he had been listening outside. 'His Royal Highness wants you to move a box from under his bed. Can you manage on your own?' she said.

He pulled a sarcastic face. 'I can manage. After all I put it there when we moved in.'

Charles was delighted when the box was hauled on to the carpet by his bedside. 'It must travel with me, and when we get to the Muti, put it beneath my bed there,' he told his servant, who bowed and said, 'As usual, sire.' It was an act of insolence which surprisingly went unreprimanded.

Charlotte was wildly curious to know what was in the box and stood staring at it but her father waved a hand in her direction and said, 'Off with you now. You must have your own packing to do. We leave here at noon.'

When she went back into the hall, the valet was still waiting outside the door. She could not help herself from stopping and saying to him, 'That box was very heavy. I couldn't shift it.'

'Money is heavy,' was the reply.

'Money?' She was astonished. The valet was sorry for her because he saw how his master exploited her and he also guessed that she often felt unwell though she managed to hide it.

'He always has a box of money beneath his bed. He says it makes him feel safe,' he told her.

I must not ask how much there is but I am sure he knows, she thought as she tried to keep her face expressionless.

'At the moment there are several hundred golden guineas in

that box as well as other coins. Sometimes he gets them out and counts them,' whispered the valet, who knew he was in the privileged position of being the only person apart from Charles who knew about this hidden fortune.

Like everybody else in the palace, he wondered how long his master would live and had already made plans to help himself to some of the bounty when death struck. If this daughter of the old man had any sense she would do the same because she deserved some return for her devoted care and he suspected that there was not much chance of her getting much from her father.

Charlotte walked slowly away with her mind racing. How shaming if her father slept every night on top of a box of golden coins but continually plagued other important people for money and accepted even the comparatively small sums which often arrived with sarcastic letters from the donors.

She remembered the straitened circumstances of her mother who had never received a groat from Charles and was forced to rely on others' charity too, especially on money from his brother the Cardinal. It was difficult not to feel angry about that.

When they arrived at the Palazzo Muti, Henry stood waiting at the top of the steps that led to the front door when his brother was carried into the courtyard in his litter. It struck him that every time he met Charles after a time apart his brother had deteriorated beyond belief.

The rheumy eyes that stared back at him from beneath an elaborate wig were those of an old and very ill man and the smell that came from him was nauseating. Henry stepped back a little to try to avoid the worst of it. As far as he was concerned, there was no question of the brothers embracing.

A quartet of servants ran forward to help Charles on to his feet and he tottered on bandaged legs as he revealed himself in his richly embroidered clothes. Henry also noticed that his face was plastered with some sort of cosmetic paste to hide his high colour.

'Welcome home, brother,' Henry cried in a falsely cheerful voice.

'Home? I hated this place. It was always so mournful even after I decorated it for that woman I married. No wonder our mother starved herself to death rather than live here,' was Charles' reply.

He cast an eye over his brother who was still as thin as a rake and dark as a native Italian. There was nothing of the aristocrat about him really, he thought in spite of his scarlet robes and the heavy jewelled crucifix round his neck.

'Where is your daughter? I am eager to meet her,' said Henry, looking around at the sweating horses and the richly curtained litter with a coronet on top in which Charles had travelled.

'She is a short distance behind. She is not a very good travel-ler because she has never been used to it. In fact I think she is scared of horses,' Charles said as a troop of people rode in with Charlotte on a white horse in the middle of them. Seeing the red-robed man on the steps with her father, she jumped to the ground and ran over to pay her respects.

With a deep curtsey she said, 'Please bless me, your grace. I am greatly in your debt because of your kindness to my mother over the years.' Without the regular payment of a pension from Henry she and Clementine would probably have starved.

It was obvious that her gratitude was genuine and Henry smiled sincerely at her and held out a hand for her to kiss. Because he appeared at first as an austere figure, she was surprised by the sweetness of his smile. She felt this man could be an ally but was too afraid of him to feel that she could take him completely into her confidence. His smile might not be so sweet if he knew she was the mother of three illegitimate children whose father was an archbishop.

In Rome Charles' health deteriorated as his doctors feared it would. The sores on his legs suppurated continually; his mind wandered more than ever and when he did recollect himself he was wickedly waspish. The apoplectic fits were more frequent and more disabling, each one leaving him more diminished and in-capable of movement.

Yet he still did not die but clung to life with the determination of a limpet. His brother sat by his bedside and looked with sorrow and pity at the wreck propped up on the pillows with the inevitable pet dog lying asleep beside him.

I hope I am spared an end like his, Henry thought sadly.

His niece stood by his side and he saw with pity that she too looked ill. Her complexion was pasty and she had lost a great deal of weight since her arrival in Rome. The poor thing was wearing herself out looking after her fractious father who would not allow her to stay away from his room for any length of time.

Even when she should have been in bed herself, she was forced to sit by him listening to the interminable tales of his own heroics which seemed to be the only thing he remembered from his ill-fated expedition of 1745.

'My dear, I fear that the next time we meet will be over my poor brother's bier,' said Henry to Charlotte when he took his farewell of her one wearisome night.

She mournfully nodded. 'I hope his suffering will not be too long,' she replied.

But both of them were in for another surprise.

Sixteen

A man on a sweating horse clattered into the courtyard of the Cardinal's palace at Frascati on the evening of the day after Christmas in 1785. He was bringing an urgent letter for the Cardinal from his niece in Rome.

'It will be as great a shock to you as it has been to me to learn that my father, your brother, was married today to one of the women of his household. Her name is Marguerite de Lussan and she was one of the attendants on his wife Louise who stayed on after Louise left,' Charlotte wrote.

The Cardinal, who was eating his supper, spluttered into his wine when he read these words. 'It's not possible. The girl must be mistaken. The last time I saw Charles he was on the point of death,' he told his lover as he passed the letter across the table.

Cesarini laughed. 'It's exactly the sort of thing he'd do. He knows everybody has been waiting for him to die for years so he keeps on going. He really is a man of iron, this Young Pretender.'

'But marrying some unknown woman! Why? He hasn't the strength to get out of bed. How can he take a wife?'

'Watch out. He'll probably produce a child as well. No wonder his daughter in Rome is worried. She must see her privileged position and hopes of inheritance disappearing in front of her eyes.'

Henry said nothing but his own hopes of being the last Stewart king were also in danger. Surely, he told himself, Charles was impotent. He hadn't even the strength to lift a spoon to his mouth the last time they met. Charlotte had to feed him, a disgusting, slobbering sight.

'But why get married? And who is this woman? I've never even heard of her,' he persisted.

'You know very well that a gaggle of adoring Jacobite ladies follow him everywhere and always have done. I'll make enquiries about her family – De Lussan, you say. At least it is an aristocratic

name, not like Walkinshaw,' said the man on the other side of the
table.

Henry wasted no time in heading for Rome, clattering over
fifteen miles of ancient road from Frascati at an enormous speed
in his magnificent carriage. He arrived at the Palazzo Muti and
found Charlotte in a state of distress.

'I knew nothing of his plans or I'd have warned you and you
might have been able to put a stop to it,' she told her uncle in
a quavering voice. Her skin was lemon coloured and there were
deep purple bags beneath her eyes.

'Where is he?' asked Henry.

'In his chamber with his wife.'

'Where was the wedding held?'

Charlotte pointed at the window. 'Over there, on the other
side of the road, in the Church of the Holy Apostle.'

Henry knew the church. 'At least he didn't have far to go,' he
said bitterly.

'He was carried across in his litter,' Charlotte told him. In fact
the first she knew of the wedding was when she saw her father,
gorgeously dressed and bewigged, being manhandled into the
litter for the short journey to the church. At the time she wondered
why he was taking so much trouble to go out to say his prayers.
It was only when he came back with Marguerite de Lussan
walking beside him that she was told what had taken place.

A devil of malice danced in Charles' eyes when he told her,
'Kiss your new stepmother, my dear.' Obviously even though
she had devoted so much time and devotion on him, he still
doubted her motives. He did not know the meaning of the
word love and he thought that self interest was the motive
behind everything ever done for him.

'I must go and meet this woman,' said Henry gravely, gathering
up his robes as he climbed the stairs.

The groom, his brother, was in bed. If he did not know what
had happened, Henry would have thought he'd never moved
since they last met. Even the dog was still there. Sitting by the
bedside however was a large, full-busted woman with a heavy
florid face who he had occasionally noticed in his brother's
entourage but had dismissed as being one of the hangers-on left
behind by Louise.

'Ah, my brother the Cardinal!' came Charles' voice from the bed when he stepped into the room. It was obvious he was enjoying himself hugely.

The woman stood up and curtseyed to Henry who found himself for once at a loss about what to say. He could not bring himself to utter congratulations but he did not want to show pique or disquiet because he knew that would delight his brother.

'I understand that you have just become my brother's wife,' he said to her. Then he looked at Charles and asked, 'Are you sure it's legally possible for you to marry again? Louise is still alive and you and she are only separated.'

Charles swept the objections away with a flick of the hand. 'Papal permission will be granted. I have the matter in hand.'

Henry switched his stare from the man in the bed to the smiling woman beside it and wondered how old she was. From her appearance she could be about forty. Too old to bear a child, he hoped.

'You have not been married before?' he asked her and she shook her head.

'No, your grace.'

'Does your family know about this?' he wanted to know and she understood that he was asking for her antecedents. 'My father is dead but he was Ferdinand d'Audibert de Lussan, a French nobleman.'

Henry nodded gravely, still wondering what bond had brought this two to the altar and she told him, 'Your brother and I share a great love of music. We often play together.'

'She is a magnificent musician. You must come and hear us performing on the viols together,' said Charles gleefully. Henry did not want to avail himself of that treat and could hardly wait to flee back to Frascati to share his news with his lover.

Before he left the Palazzo Muti however he sought out Charlotte and assured her, 'This strange business will have no effect on you or on the money I send to your mother, my dear. Stay here with him because he will still need your care. I don't think his new wife has much inclination for nursing.'

Charlotte promised to stay. After all where could she go? She had invested too much of her life in her father to give up now.

At least he continued to repay her by continuing to go out with her to many social events and treating her with great respect, even referring to her in public as La Pretendente.

She was also still allowed to wear the Sobieski jewels because such fripperies did not suit Marguerite.

She saw her new stepmother only rarely, and usually only when Charles and his new wife staged a little concert for their own pleasure because both were skilled musicians and he seemed to have been regenerated even more since his marriage.

Sitting with her eyes closed listening to their music was a time of peace and contemplation for Charlotte but it also made her sad for the music took her away from Rome, back to her mother and her beloved children. How big was her baby son now? she wondered, and her arms ached with the desire to hold him again.

In fact she often ached all over and a terrible dejecting tiredness seemed to have engulfed her. There was a nagging pain in her stomach that never seemed to go away and she thought it was caused by sorrow and longing for the people she loved.

'I have to keep on going. It cannot last much longer,' she thought, opening her eyes and seeing Charles slump forward in one of his transient fits at the end of the piece they were playing.

When Marguerite stood up to bend over him, Charlotte saw with surprise how much the woman's stomach stuck out. 'Is it possible that she is pregnant? Is she having a child?' she thought in consternation and the shock was so terrible that she felt herself go faint. It was a struggle not to fall from the chair herself.

Henry was equally horrified when she passed on her suspicions to him but, suave as ever, he managed to winkle the truth out of Marguerite and Charles. She was indeed expecting a child and it would be born in the autumn.

'If I have a son at last it will be another claimant to the throne,' exulted Charles who was still disregarding the possibility that his marriage was invalid.

'I hope the poor boy will never be saddled with the Stewart ambitions because they are hopeless. Too much blood and too many tears have been shed over the pointlessness of it all. The time has passed,' said Henry sharply but Charles did not want to hear him. He was off again in his Jacobite fantasy.

At the end of September, Marguerite, who was enormously pregnant, went to stay with her sister in another part of Rome because, she said, she did not want her husband upset by any fuss about her delivery.

A boy was born on October 6th and as an infant of two days, he was carried in to be viewed by his bedbound father.

'He looks like a fine specimen. I will call him Edward James,' said Charles but he did not offer to hold the child who was plump and healthy-looking.

Charlotte, who was also in the room and watching the scene, felt a stab of anguish as she looked at the baby in its tight swaddling clothes. Her own son was not much bigger than that when she had to leave him behind with her mother. For how much longer? she wondered.

Henry made his appearance the next day and gave a cursory glance at the new baby. His main interest was, however, the mother. 'I hope you realize that my brother has not yet been divorced from his wife Louise,' he said to her.

She looked at him blankly and he wondered how much she understood of what he was saying.

'There will be questions about your son's legitimacy,' he added.

'His father accepts him,' she replied.

'He also accepts his daughter Charlotte though she is illegitimate.'

'What are you trying to say?' asked Marguerite.

'You must know that my brother is dying. The doctors are amazed he has lasted so long. Another fit could kill him.'

'His doctors have been saying that for a long time.'

Henry looked exasperated. 'There's no use pretending. When he dies, I will accept your son and become his guardian but there must be no question of him or anyone else staking a claim on his behalf to the English, Scottish and Irish crowns. That has to stop.'

Marguerite nodded. 'I understand. But he is the only son of a royal claimant. What sort of title will he have?'

'We will call him Count Stuarton but only if you agree that he will never lay any claims to royalty.'

'And what sort of settlement will be made on him?' She was nothing if not practical.

'I will leave him well provided for in my will and though my brother pleads poverty, he has a considerable fortune, including very valuable jewels from our mother's family. Your son will get all these,' Henry told her.

'I don't know what you think of me but I assure you that I did not marry your brother for selfish or greedy reasons. I have always felt affection for him, especially after his wife left him. It was his idea that we should marry and I did not intend to have a child – I thought I was too old – but I have been blessed with this boy and he is a blessing from God as far as I am concerned. I have no wish to expose him to the perils of a royal existence. I want him to live a normal life,' she said slowly and Henry felt a tremor of sympathy for her.

Till then he'd suspected her of marrying Charles through ambition or self interest but now he was having second thoughts. Perhaps she was genuinely fond of the old devil, unlikely as that seemed. Charles had always been able to cast a spell over women and it seemed that even now, in his decrepitude, it was still effective.

'He's drifting into death. The person who is closest to him and who he needs most is his daughter. You must see that. This is not a house for a child to grow up in. Take the baby back to your sister's house and I'll make sure you are both well provided for,' Henry told her.

She knew that what he said was true. With every day that passed Charles was losing his grip on life and he had no real interest in his son. In fact at times he seemed to forget about the child's existence.

'I will do as you wish,' she told the Cardinal and moved away to raise her son alone, taking him occasionally to be viewed by his father who did not seem to know either of them.

But still he did not die.

Fit followed fit. Within six months he was paralysed down one side and could only make mumbling noises. The one person who understood what he was trying to say was Charlotte who hovered over his bed and brought what he wanted. As she cared for him, she spoke softly and he looked up dumbly at her with his eyes as sardonic as ever.

Christmas 1787 was a miserable time in the Palazzo Muti and

at the beginning of January more seizures rendered him totally immobile, unable even to mutter any longer.

Doctors stood round his bed and marvelled at his resilience. 'He should have been dead months ago,' said one to Charlotte.

She replied, 'It would have been more merciful, I think.'

The man stared back at her and said, 'There's no point us dosing him any more. If someone was to put a pillow over his face, he would go to sleep forever.'

She shook her head. 'I know but I cannot do it. It would be a mortal sin.'

She looked exhausted and the doctor felt he had to warn her, 'You must rest. Caring for him is wearing you out.'

There were tears in her eyes when she looked back at him. 'He is my father and I love him. No one else cares for him as I do. When it's all over I will be able to rest.'

Charles died on January 30th with Charlotte holding his hand. His brother had given him the last rites and when it was certain that life had left him, she laid his hand back on his chest and walked out of the room. Her legs were so feeble that she could hardly stand and there was a terrible pain in her stomach. She went to bed, dosed with potions from the doctors, and slept for a day and a night.

Though Bonnie Prince Charlie died on January 30th, his brother Henry deliberately delayed the announcement for twenty-four hours because the 30th was reckoned to be an unlucky day for the Stewarts as it was the day that Charles I was executed in Whitehall, London, and all their troubles began.

The funeral at Frascati, presided over by Henry, was magnificent. Charles had wanted to be buried in St Peter's Basilica beside his father and mother but the Pope was not prepared to give permission for that immediately, though he relented later and then the body was moved to Rome where it later lay beneath the marble sculpture by Canova. Because the birth of his son was known to only a few people, his official heir was his brother Henry who began signing letters as Henry IX and went out to touch people suffering from the King's Evil.

Epilogue

Charlotte did not attend her father's funeral because she was very ill, suffering from a severe disturbance of the liver. She fretted as she lay in bed because she longed to be able to get up and ride back to France and the people she loved. Her weakness was totally debilitating however and she fretfully asked her doctors, 'When will I be well enough to travel?'

'Soon, soon,' they assured her but outside her room, they shook their heads because they knew that the illness would kill her. It was slow but inexorable and dragged on week after week, taking its deadly toll on her with every day that passed.

'How cruel that she will die so soon after caring for her father for all this time,' said one of the doctors to Henry when he came to visit his niece.

'Is her death certain?' her uncle asked in a sorrowful tone because he too recognized the sacrifice she had made.

'Sadly so. She has cancer of the liver.'

'But she is only thirty-six years old!'

'Death does not spare the young, Your Grace.'

'Does she know?'

'No, she keeps on saying that she wants to go back to France to see her mother again.'

Henry nodded. 'They were always very close. Can you do anything to help her get there?'

'We will try but she is very wasted and if she journeys it will have to be in short stages.'

'Then let us try to arrange that,' said Henry and went in to speak to Charlotte. 'Your doctor thinks that you will be able to travel soon if you take the journey slowly,' he told her.

Relief filled her face. 'Thank God. I am longing to see my mother . . . and I'm afraid I have a secret. I was the mother of three small children when I came to live with my father. I am sorry to have kept them secret but I wanted to tell you now.'

He was not too shocked for he was a worldly man who

realized everyone had secrets. 'You gave a lot up for my brother,' he said.

She looked up at him out of sunken eyes. 'I did not do it for selfish reasons. I came because I always loved him. He was my father.'

Henry nodded. He knew that Charles had left a reasonable but not large sum of money to Charlotte in his will and he himself intended to continue paying her mother's pension.

'Have you made a will?' he asked and she shuddered.

'No, no, I'm afraid that if I was to make a will it would hurry on my death. I must see the people I love first. I must go back.'

He was sorry to hear that, because from what the doctors told him it was unlikely that she would be able to complete the journey to France. Instead of urging her to put aside her fear, he asked gently, 'Can I help you with your travel arrangements?'

'I intend to take it slowly. I have a friend, the Marchesa Julia Lambortina Bovia who is living in Bologna, and she will let me stay there with her on the first stage of my journey,' Charlotte told him.

'Then you must travel in the style that is appropriate to your status. I'll arrange for transport and an escort,' he said and when he left the room he was afraid that he would never see his brother's daughter again.

Charlotte was determined to go back but by the time she arrived at her friend's home, the Palazzo Vizzani Sanguinetti in Bologna, she was desperately ill and in great pain. For weeks she lay weakly in bed and her friend Julia spent hours sitting beside her.

One day she burst into tears and groaned, 'I know now that I have been deceiving myself. I cannot go on any longer. I'm dying. Oh how I have longed to see my mother and my dear children again, but even that is being denied me.'

Julia wept too because she knew that what Charlotte said was true.

'I must make my will. The Cardinal told me to when I was in Rome but I was afraid. Now I know I have no time to waste,' whispered the sick woman.

A notary was fetched and she gave him her instructions. Her mother was to have 50,000 livres and an annuity of 15,000 a year from the money Charles had left his daughter. Charlotte knew she had enough funds to cover it because, almost with his last words, her father told her to take the box of coins from beneath his bed and so she was able to leave bequests to every member of her household. No one was left out.

The day after she signed her will, she lapsed into unconsciousness and died two days later, just a year after her father. She was buried with a modest ceremony in the Church of San Biagio in Bologna.

The will was sent on to Clementine who wept when she unfolded it and saw her daughter's shaky last signature.

'Fate has been cruel to us,' she sobbed and her mind ranged back to the time when she first knew Charles and was so entranced by him that she was prepared to defy convention and follow him anywhere he went.

Though Henry was Charles' direct heir and the bulk of the Stewart estate had been left to him, he knew nothing about the box of gold that Charles took with him everywhere until he read his niece's will. Then he was furious and reluctant to part with any more cash for Clementine from Charlotte's will.

'My brother instructed me to make provision for his infant son and now I have to deal with the demands of his mistress as well,' he fumed and ignored Clementine's letters asking for her inheritance to be sent on.

She persevered however because she had Charlotte's three children to bring up and in the end her persistence wore him down.

'I will pay you the money that your daughter left to you but only if you are prepared to sign a deed renouncing any more claims, now or in the future, on my brother's estate,' he wrote to her.

As usual Clementine acquiesced and signed the deed of quittance, as it was called. She needed the money badly.

When the French Revolution began to rage through the country, she took her grandchildren to Switzerland where they grew up and where she died in 1802 at the age of eighty-two.

Charlotte's three children had hardly any memory of their mother except from the stories told to them by their grandmother. The little boy, Charles Edward, who had only been an infant when his mother went to Italy, was given into the care of his father when he reached the age of needing an education and he was brought up by the aristocratic Rohan family who also took an interest in the girls, both of whom went on to make good marriages with Polish noblemen.

As an adult Charlotte's son became an officer in the Russian army, and later a general with the Austrian forces. He was very proud of his link with his grandfather Prince Charles Edward Stewart and in 1854 he made a visit to Scotland to see the land of his ancestors but the coach in which he was travelling overturned on the road between Perth and Dunkeld and he was killed outright. His body lies in Dunkeld cathedral.

After Charlotte, the next person whose life had been involved with Charles Edward Stewart to die was Flora Macdonald. She never regained her health after returning to her beloved home at Penduin on Skye.

Worn out by travel and pain, her life drew slowly to its end but she was consoled by the loving attendance of her remaining children, Anne, Fanny, Charles and James. John, widowed by the terrible fever that reaped its cruel harvest among young women in the tropics, was still in India and faithfully sending money to his parents at home. Only three years after settling into her own home again, with her beloved Allan beside her, Flora died in the Prince's bed in 1790.

As proud of his wife as ever, Allan was determined that she should go out in style with a magnificent funeral and her coffin was carried to Kilmuir cemetery in the middle of an immense cavalcade of plaid-wearing men marching behind a team of pipers playing the Coronach, the great lament of the Gaels. Then all the mourners went back to Penduin and held a wake that lasted for three days.

Without her, Allan lost his zest for life and two years later he was laid to rest beside her.

Louise and Alfieri never separated after their reunion at Colmar and lived openly together but never married. They moved first to Paris where Louise set up another salon to which people flocked in the hope of meeting her famous playwright lover. When news came that Charles had died, the couple felt it was safe enough to return to Italy.

It was time to leave Paris anyway because the Revolution had just begun and they only escaped from the city in time. As they were riding away to Calais, a troop of National Guard revolutionaries were advancing on their house to arrest them because Louise was known to be a friend of the Queen.

The upheaval also meant that she lost her French pension of 60,000 livres a year but she still had her financial settlement of 6000 crowns per annum from Charles' estate and Alfieri was at the peak of his earning powers with enough money to buy the fine Palazzo Gianfigliazzi in Florence where they lived in high style, and Louise set up yet another salon.

'Now that my husband is dead, I'm no longer bound by the terms of the deed of separation,' she told her friends in explanation of a total refurbishment of her new home for which she bought china and plate decorated with the royal arms of Great Britain and Ireland.

The people who flocked to her salon were ordered to refer to her as 'Your Majesty' and instructed on how to bow themselves out backwards from her presence without falling over.

When challenged with self aggrandizement by some brave critics, she only laughed and said, 'For the nine years that I lived with that man I was totally wretched. Now I am getting some recompense for the misery he put me through.'

Charles' brother Henry was no longer in close contact with her but he kept an eye on how she was living. 'People tell me that she's grown very fat,' he told Cesarini when they were discussing Louise.

'She was never thin and she is always eating sweetmeats so she cannot expect to become a sylph,' was the laughing reply.

'She has a very vulgar German streak but in a way I always liked her. There was something honourable about her,' mused Henry.

'I wonder why she never married her lover,' said Cesarini.

'In the beginning she couldn't because she'd have lost her separation allowance from my brother if she married again. Later on I don't suppose it mattered to either of them for she was never a maternal woman. When I bribed her to stay childless I could have saved my money.' They both laughed, and when Henry died in 1821 Louise was surprised to find that he had left her the legacy of a gold watch as a token of his respect.

Louise and Alfieri stayed faithful to each other but as the years went on, he became increasingly eccentric though as prolific in output as before.

'I'm tired of writing tragedies. Now I intend to write only comedies,' he told her and they poured from him in a steady stream. When he was involved in his writing he had a notice propped against his front door in Florence warning visitors to stay away because he was busy.

Though his comedies were not as well written as his tragedies, they were well received by a worshipping public and he kept on working until his death, which was sudden and unexpected.

Though fit through constant riding and whip thin, he was felled by a heart attack at the age of fifty-four as he sat in his armchair at home in 1803. Louise was inconsolable but determined that the man she loved for so long should go out of this world in the greatest style possible.

Alfieri was buried in the Basilica of Santa Croce in Florence and his grave was sited between those of Michelangelo and Machiavelli.

'He is in distinguished company, which is only what he deserves,' she said at his funeral mass. Then she also commissioned the sculptor Canova to design him a magnificent tomb which cost her the vast sum of 10,000 scudi.

Louise lived on, growing fatter and more feted by foreign visitors who flocked to her salon in Florence. She found herself another man, much younger than herself this time, an artist called Francois Fabre. He was an up-and-coming painter in 1793 when Alfieri commissioned him to paint her portrait and it turned out to be an excellent likeness, showing her as slightly dishevelled but sensual looking, lusciously plump with her beautiful hands spread out in her lap in all their glory.

When Alfieri died, Fabre was constantly by her side and very quickly moved into her Palazzo. They lived together till she died of dropsy at the age of seventy-one in 1823. Her will left all her possessions to Fabre.

When Henry Benedict, Cardinal Duke of York, died in 1807, he was the longest-serving cardinal in the Catholic church. He died in Frascati with Cesarini holding his hand and was buried in St

Peter's Basilica beneath the Canova monument that was erected to mark the graves of his parents.

His brother Charles Edward was also laid to rest there a few years after his death when the Pope relented and agreed to let him lie in the Vatican.

In his will Charles acknowledged his son Edward James and created him Count Stuarton, 2nd Duke of Albany. Henry was appointed regent and the remains of the Sobieski jewels were to be divided between Edward and Charlotte, who died before she could be given them.

The little boy was carefully tended by his mother who was afraid that if too much fuss was made about his claim to the Stewart pretensions, he would be in danger. The Hanoverian monarchy of Great Britain ignored the child and successfully brushed his name out of existence and when Cardinal Henry, who persisted in styling himself Henry IX, died in 1807 the Stewart family succession was declared extinct and a statement made to that effect in the House of Commons.

Edward James lived a comfortable but quiet life and had no ambition to equal the grandeur of his ancestors. He married an Italian noblewoman and in 1809 produced a son called Henry Edward, dying in 1845, a century after his father's ill-fated attempt to raise a Jacobite rebellion in Scotland. Henry Edward, his son, died in 1869. There have been various Stewart claimants since but their days of glory have long passed.